DON'T!

"Hey, Jason," came my brother's voice out of the speaker.

"Whatever you do, DON'T lose me this lease. It's the best deal in town. Sell your friends, but hang onto that apartment.

"I'll send you a postcard from London. See ya.

"Oh, yeah — Plotnick doesn't know all three of you are going to be living here. I told him it was just you. Fake it. Say the others are houseguests or something."

Other books by
GORDON KORMAN

point

LOSING JOE'S PLACE

Gordon Korman

SCHOLASTIC INC.
New York Toronto London Auckland Sydney

ISBN 0-590-42769-5

Copyright © 1990 by Gordon Korman Enterprises, Inc. All rights reserved. Published by Scholastic Inc. POINT is a registered trademark of Scholastic Inc.

24   5 6 7 8/0

For Megan Sarah Pekilis
from The Godfather
                    —*GK*

SEPTEMBER

One

Joe Cardone, twenty-two, bodybuilder, big, mad, and my brother, screeched into the driveway in his black Camaro, roared in the front door, and bellowed,

"Where is he?"

The "he" was me, Jason Cardone, sixteen, weakling, small, scared, and hiding in my room.

Joe had just flown in from Europe that morning, and was ticked off enough to drive a hundred and twenty miles from Toronto to Owen Sound just to kill me. I knew he'd be coming after me, but I figured he'd spend at least a couple of days in his downtown Toronto apartment, which he loved so much, and which he had to move out of by the 30th, thanks to me.

What fool did away with locks on bedroom doors? What good were parents if they were going to be out shopping when their child needed protection?

Joe burst into my room like a thundering herd of buffalo. I almost swallowed the book I was pretending to read.

"Hi, Joe. Great tan."

"I'll tan you, you little jerkface! What have you done to me?"

"Aw, Joe, I'm really sorry — "

"*Sorry?!*" Joe was wearing a sleeveless shirt, and when he yelled, the veins bulged out of his arm muscles. Even his biceps had biceps. "You *lost* my apartment! The best deal in Toronto! And *I* had it! And *you* lost it!"

"But Joe — "

"*Shut up!*" His tan was purpling rapidly. "When I let you and your two sleazy friends live in my place for the summer, did I play nanny and come up with a whole pack of rules — 'do this,' 'don't do that'?" He slammed a hammerlike fist down on the desk, sending my model of the U.S.S. *Enterprise* shattering to the floor. "*No!* I said *one thing*! 'Don't lose me my lease!' *Was that so hard?*"

Fifty perfectly good sob stories formed in my mind. But even if I could get a word in edgewise, what would I say? It was true. Don Champion, Ferguson Peach, and I had taken over the apartment while Joe was in Europe — a position of supreme trust. We were honored that my brother would have such faith in us. And what did he get for his faith? Evicted. That's what. It didn't matter to Joe that it wasn't our fault. What did he care that we were victims of circumstance? He grabbed me by the collar and the seat of my pants and frog-marched me to the telephone. "Okay, dogmeat! You call up Frick and Frack and tell them to get their dumb butts over here! I want to have a *discussion* about how I used to have an apartment, and I don't have one anymore because of three idiots!"

What could I do? I picked up the phone. . . .

JUNE

Two

Ferguson Peach leaned forward and tapped the taxi driver on the shoulder. "Pardon me, sir, but after you let us off, you should go straight to a repair shop and see about your motor supports. They're very weak."

The man glared at him in the rearview mirror. "Who are you — Mr. Goodwrench? Mind your own business, kid. I've been a cabbie for twenty years, and there's nothing wrong with this car."

Don Champion nudged me. "Is he going to do this all summer?"

Ferguson and Don were both best friends of mine, but they weren't really friends of each other.

Now, in the cab headed for 1 Pitt Street, seemed a stupid time for me to notice it.

"I mean, we made it!" Don continued, motioning all around us. "Downtown Toronto. Bright lights, big city, and the best summer of our lives!"

The Peach shrugged. "We'll be working. If we stayed in Owen Sound, we could spend our summer on the beach."

I couldn't help laughing. "You'd die of boredom lying on the beach, Ferguson. You can't fix a beach."

"You can dredge."

"Joe's the greatest guy in the world to let us move into his place this summer," said Don. "Let's face it, Owen Sound is okay, but we're not babies anymore. We need to see the world."

Don is a pretty confident guy. Back home in Owen Sound, he's kind of like Mr. Wonderful. He's the best hockey player in town, and high school president two years in a row, and he dates all the greatest girls. With a record like that, who wouldn't look forward to each new day?

"There's a difference between the world and the inside of a plastics factory." If life was a picnic, Ferguson Peach was rain. And ants.

"We'll do a lot more than just work," I argued. "When school starts again in September, all those other bozos who spent the summer hanging around home will be like ten-year-olds compared to us. We'll be men!"

Don challenged Ferguson. "If this whole thing is so lousy, why are you here?"

Ferguson cocked an eyebrow. "Because everyone I know is going to be at Joe's place."

In a way, Ferguson and Don were in perfect agreement about our summer plans. Ferguson didn't really want to come along, and Don didn't really want him to, either. But we needed a third to split up the rent. And, to Ferguson's credit, he gave the most spectacular performance of any of us on the day we hit up our parents for permission to go out into the world.

We all tackled our folks at the same hour on the same night, so that when they stopped yelling at us and went to phone each other, the lines would be busy. That's when we could say "Well, ———— 's parents are letting *him* go." Because of Ferguson's artistry, the Peaches caved in first, followed by the Champions. The Cardones, my pair, held out to the end.

"You're too young," was my mother's big argument. When I'm eighty and she's a hundred and nine, this will still make sense to her.

"If I trust Jason, you should, too," said my brother Joe, who would have to find another tenant if the deal fell through. "I mean, it's *my* apartment."

Then my mother shifted into overdrive, and by the time the dust cleared, not only was *I* too young, but so was Joe. And she expected him to cancel his trip to Europe, give up his apartment, and move back home. Joe bailed out on me there, but by that time, the Peaches and the Champions had both said yes. Mom didn't have a leg to stand on.

Mr. Wonderful put his arm around my shoulder. "Jason, I refuse to let this guy spoil our trip. I happen to know that it is mathematically impossible for this summer to be anything but perfect."

Ferguson snorted. "Mathematically? How does that work?"

Don was smug. "One, everybody knows that Joe Cardone is the coolest guy ever to come out of Owen Sound. He wouldn't live in just any old dump, so the apartment is going to be amazing. Two — Toronto is an awesome city for young single guys. Three — my uncle's going to treat us great in his factory, so the jobs'll be fantastic. That's three for a good time, zero for a bad time; we've already got a hat trick, and we haven't even moved in yet."

As we made our way through the traffic, a very weird feeling started to take hold of my stomach. It wasn't fear; I didn't want to go back. I was just so pumped up about the summer that I was operating at double speed while the rest of the world was in slow motion. When the guy at the Indy 500 says, "Gentlemen, start your engines," all the drivers at the line feel exactly like I did in that cab.

Don was going to Toronto to have fun and, knowing him, he would have lots of it, every day. Ferguson was going mostly because of me, and Toronto wouldn't make much difference to him. Neither would Mars. But for me this summer was the only game in town. With my overprotective parents, this was my one chance to prove I could make it on my own. Screw up, and I'd be lucky to see the light of day before I started university.

Most parents baby their first kid, and then learn to let go with the others. My folks got it backwards. They allowed Joe a lot of independence, and when he quit college, moved to the big city, and became a bodybuilder, they said to themselves, *"Mistake!"* Since then, Mom and Dad have been all over me like a cheap suit. They hadn't even let me come to Toronto to *visit* Joe. The fact that I was now on my way to *live* in his place was a major miracle.

"You'll be back in a week, flat broke, with your tail between your legs." This was my father's parting shot on the platform in Owen Sound. I knew right then that, even if I died in Toronto, my last act would be to take a magic marker and write across my chest, *Do Not Return Until September 1st*.

Don and I were rubbernecking out the windows, pointing and yammering about our new town. We couldn't wait to see Joe's apartment, which was going to be our bachelor pad. Because we were on the alert, we couldn't help noticing that the scenery was getting older, dingier, and more run-down. The sleek chrome and gunmetal buildings were gone, replaced by tenement houses, and the taxi's shocks began to protest the uneven pavement.

Don got philosophical. "It's a good lesson for us to drive through this area right on our first day. We're moving to the city for all its good stuff, but we should remember that it can be a pretty tough place for the poor."

At that instant, our taxi veered in to the curb, and the driver popped the meter, and announced, "One Pitt Street."

Ferguson gawked. "Oh, my God — *we're* the poor!"

I could hardly speak. "Are you — positive this is the right place? Could there be — another Pitt Street?"

The cabbie laughed. "This is the only one there is, kid. Take it or leave it."

"Well, obviously there's been some mistake,"

said Don. Things always turned out great for Mr. Wonderful, so he figured that the slum we'd arrived at was just a misunderstanding. "You see, the place we're looking for is a great apartment. Probably a big tower, lots of chrome, doorman, pool, health club — that kind of thing."

The driver looked disgusted. "The guy asked for 1 Pitt Street, and here it is. Are you getting out, or what?"

We got out. And when the cab pulled away, we must have looked like three total jerks, standing on the broken sidewalk, surrounded by our stupid luggage.

"So this is Joe's place," said the Peach. If sarcasm was electricity, that guy would be a power station.

I groped for words. There was no denying that the neighborhood was a dump, consisting of beat-up row houses, pawnshops, cheap bars, empty storefronts, an abandoned furniture factory, and a large field of electrical towers that made Pitt Street into a dead end. It was awful — dull, drab, dirty, ugly. How could any living creature thrive and be happy in such a place?

But, on the other hand, my brother Joe thought he had the greatest apartment in the world. To him, paying six hundred and eighty-five bucks a month to live *here* was an incredible bargain. Obviously I was missing something because I'd grown up in Owen Sound and had no concept of city life.

I gave Ferguson and Don my best superior look. "You guys know nothing about cool. What a couple of small-town hicks. In the city, people fight to get into a great area like this. It's where the artists and musicians hang out. Don't you ever watch TV?''

Mr. Wonderful scanned our surroundings with an appraiser's eye. "I'm starting to get the hang of it. It isn't slummy; it's — funky."

"And trendy," I added.

But when I think back to my first view of 1 Pitt Street, the only word that comes to mind is "rat-trap." Picture three stories of crumbling red brick, peeling white paint, and the Olympiad Delicatessen. Joe had mentioned there was a deli on his street, but he'd never said he lived over it. It was the whole first floor, with a string of salamis hanging in the dusty window. There a sign read:

BREAKFAST — LUNCH — DINNER
PARTY TRAYS
HUB CAPS

It wasn't easy, but I smiled. "The best is yet to come, guys. Let's check it out."

I already had Joe's spare keys, and I found the one that fit the outside door. As it turned out, the lock was broken. The door swung wide, and I led a somewhat reluctant Ferguson and Don into 1 Pitt Street. My plan was to rave about everything. I went on and on about how terrific ancient linoleum was. I loved the rickety stairs that were covered in so much dirt that, if someone accidentally spilled a packet of seeds, the following year he'd have geraniums. I was really impressed by the peeling wallpaper and the battered framed photograph of several old men dancing with each other.

Ferguson couldn't hold it in. "This building is a structural nightmare."

"Sure," said Don sarcastically. "The cab was supposed to explode, too, remember?"

Apartment 2C was directly over the deli in front, down a long, dingy hallway. I had to admit I was expecting the worst, but stepping into Joe's place was like entering the twenty-first century.

It was all one room, but big, and boy, had my brother ever decked it out! The place was wired for sound, with speakers all over. It was impossible to tell which ones were hooked up to the stereo, and which to the wide-screen TV and VCR. He had it all — from Nintendo to darts. At opposite ends of the room, Nerf basketball hoops were tacked to the walls. Between them was a "court," free of rugs and furniture, complete with tip-off circle and 3-point lines.

When you have muscles like my brother, you enjoy getting your picture taken a lot, so the decor was mostly photographs. Amid the snapshots were some of the calendars he'd posed for. Throughout his career, Joe had flexed his way through every month except April. (My birthday's in April. I've searched for some kind of meaning for this, but so far no luck.)

I threw myself onto the leather couch and sank three inches into the stuffing. Joe was right. He did have a fantastic apartment. Not what we'd expected, but definitely great. Only — something didn't seem right.

Don put it into words. "Why's it so dark in here?"

We investigated. There was only one window,

and it was in the bathroom. That made the living area as dim as a church, while the people on Pitt Street had a spectacular floor to ceiling view of our toilet.

"Very amateurish," said Ferguson, shaking his head.

Don reddened. "Is there anything, oh expert of the world, that you actually approve of?"

Ferguson thought it over. "Stonehenge," he said finally.

"Stonehenge?"

"It was very well designed."

"Joe knows how to live, but he's such a flake," I said. "First, he forgets to pick us up at the train station. Second, he isn't even here to show us where we can put our stuff. Third, there's no note, no nothing."

"Let's hope he remembers to go to Europe," put in Ferguson.

"I mean, look at this place!" I went on, warming to the subject. "Probably $20,000 worth of electronics, and I can't see five books. With every barbell he lifts, a few more brain cells turn into muscle!"

We'd probably still be standing there waiting for Joe if Don hadn't noticed that the message light on the telephone answering machine was flashing. I leaned over and hit play.

"Hey, Jason," came my brother's voice out of the speaker. *"Sorry I couldn't meet you guys, but my flight was pushed up by two days. Isn't the place great? You guys are going to have a ball, but watch out for Plot-*

nick, the landlord. He's kind of funny about certain things. The car's parked on the street just down from the deli. Here are the keys.

"Whatever you do, DON'T lose me this lease. It's the best deal in town. Sell your friends, but hang onto that apartment.

"I'll send you a postcard from London. See ya.

"Oh, yeah — Plotnick doesn't know all three of you are going to be living here. I told him it was just you. Fake it. Say the others are houseguests or something."

"Houseguests?" Don repeated. "For three months?"

"Impossible," said the Peach. "You can't be a houseguest in a place with no windows. We're caveguests."

All this was lost on me. My attention was fixed on the car keys lying beside the answering machine, glinting in the lone shaft of sunlight threading the needle all the way from the bathroom.

To go from driving my mother's rickety station wagon to Joe's Camaro was like being promoted directly from training wheels to the space shuttle. The Camaro was ten years old, but my brother kept it in mint condition. We seemed to glide along the road like a hovercraft. I hung my arm casually out the window, waving at everybody and anybody. The paint job was dark and lustrous — we must have looked like an aerodynamic black hole cruising down Bathurst Street.

We didn't get a chance to test the 350 horses

under the hood because, about fifty yards from Joe's place, we got stuck in a traffic jam. We inched ahead for about twenty minutes before passing the cause of it all. It was the taxi that had brought us from the train station, sitting immobilized in the right-hand lane. Six feet behind it lay the smouldering engine, spark plugs and all. The driver Ferguson had told to get his motor supports checked was negotiating with the tow truck operator.

"I don't like to say 'I told you so . . .' " began Ferguson.

"Then don't," snapped Don.

The Peach was making a sketch on a file card of several possible expressway routes to alleviate traffic. Don was flaked out in the back, leafing through *The Toronto Star*, searching for ways to spend our first day in the big city. It wasn't a tough job. Everything sounded great.

We took in the afternoon baseball game, and watched the Blue Jays take the White Sox into extra innings before blowing them away in the 12th. Don insisted that we needed new clothes so we wouldn't look like hayseeds. That meant shopping — which I usually hate, but that day in Toronto I really got into it. Now possessing cool wardrobes, we required cool haircuts, so Don and I blew a bundle at this fancy stylist's place. Don looked hip, but when I checked the mirror, I couldn't shake the feeling that I had been in a knife fight where my opponent had cut off both sides of my head. At that point, the Peach returned from the bookstore with his only purchase of the excursion — *An Illustrated History of Stonehenge*.

We were ready to call it a day after a trip up the

CN Tower when we found out that Electric Catfish was playing at Maple Leaf Gardens, and there were still tickets left. You don't pass up a chance to see a big-time rock concert when you come from Owen Sound. This forced us to have dinner downtown, and Don picked a Serbo-Croatian restaurant where we ordered the weirdest things on the menu. This included — and I'm *not* kidding — stewed crab-grass. There Ferguson sealed his traffic sketch in an envelope and addressed it to the mayor of Toronto. He mailed it outside the Burger King, where we went for some real food.

The concert was amazing, and we were so wired up, we rented seven ninja movies. The night was a blur of poker, Nerf basketball, and ninja attacks. I estimate we got to sleep around seven A.M.

My parents called at seven-thirty. I feel like I dreamed the whole conversation. I yawned out that everything was fine and Joe was on his way to London. Ferguson and Don threw pillows at me. I had lost the bet, as I knew I would. The guy whose folks were the first to call had to clean the bathroom all summer. Way to go, Mom.

She sounded suspicious. "Jason, are you getting enough sleep?"

"No," I said honestly. "Somebody phoned at seven-thirty on a Sunday morning. Can you believe that?" Parents have no sense of humor.

We had just gotten back to sleep when the phone rang again. Mrs. Peach; seven forty-five. And Don's mom was on the line at eight-ten.

"Is that everybody?" moaned Ferguson.

We counted noses and phone calls, and agreed that it was safe to go back to sleep.

When we finally woke up, it was two-thirty in the afternoon.

Don yawned hugely. "Did my mother phone a few hours ago?"

"*Everybody's* mother phoned," I amended. "Just don't ask me what we told them."

"Yours was first," Ferguson reminded me. "And by the way, I like my toilet to really sparkle."

Don sprang to his feet and stretched. "Come on! Let's get out there and do it all over again! Yesterday was amazing!"

"Here's something to amaze you," put in Ferguson, making quick calculations in a notebook. "We're $300 poorer."

My first thought was *we've been robbed*! "Oh, no! We *spent* that much? How?"

We gathered around the paper and gawked. As usual, the Peach was right on target. Between the concert and baseball tickets, purchases, food, hairdos and parking, we'd blown $317.45 in all. At a pace of three hundred bucks a day, this summer was going to cost us over twenty grand, not including rent. So much for not making it in the big city. We were going to have room and board for as long as we wanted it, and more — with bars on the windows.

"Give me that!" Don snatched the notebook from Ferguson and began crossing out vigorously. "Scratch all the one-time expenses, like the clothes and the hair, and take away all the stuff we did just because it was our first day, and things we got

suckered on, but now we know better, and *voilà!*"
He held the result in front of the Peach.

"Dinner for three at Burger King, $9.50," read Ferguson. Don looked proud.

"Forget it." I grabbed the notebook and tossed it onto the beanbag chair. "Let's continue our tour of the city. Today we go to everything that's either cheap or free."

We headed down to the car.

"I don't know how safe this is," said Ferguson on the staircase. "I think the supporting wood's almost rotted out."

"It's holding *you* up," snapped Don. "That's a miracle right there." Ferguson is a little chunky, but definitely not what you'd call fat.

"The building probably went up in the fifties," the Peach decided. "Which means the wood should be replaced — based on average maintenance, and humidity — "

"Shut up!" warned Don.

" . . . in the next three or four years. Of course, this architectural style began as early as 1941, in which case the stairs would become a hazard" — he paused again, calculating — "now."

No sooner was the word out of his mouth than a basketball-sized hole opened up under Don's foot, and his leg disappeared to the thigh.

"Yep, 1941."

When we lifted Don and his leg out, he was looking at Ferguson as if to say, *He's a witch! Burn him!*

"Don't worry, guys," I stepped in. "We can mention this to the landlord when we go to introduce

22

ourselves. He'll be happy no one was hurt."

We stepped outside into the hot afternoon and scanned Pitt Street for the Camaro. I frowned. In all the excitement yesterday, I'd forgotten where I'd parked the —

"Hey, Jason. Didn't we leave it right here?" Don was pointing to a spot in front of the deli.

My heart stopped. In the line of parked vehicles was an empty space just about the size of an aerodynamic black hole.

Oh, no.

"Don't worry," said Ferguson sarcastically. "Filing stolen vehicle reports is part of life in the big city."

Don and I glared at him. We were standing in front of 1 Pitt Street, where a police officer had just finished taking our report about Joe's car being gone.

"This isn't funny," I said.

"That cop sure didn't seem too upset," Don observed.

"What did you expect him to do?" asked Ferguson. "Weep? Tear his hair? Drag Lake Ontario?"

"Ferguson's got a point," I said. "After all, it's just a car. And it's insured. We'll probably get it back, but if we don't, the insurance money will buy Joe another one. We can't panic about this kind of thing. Meanwhile, we'll take buses and subways. With the traffic, it's just as fast."

"Right," said Don. "City people never lose their cool, because anything can happen in the city.

Why, do you realize that, at any second, something amazing could happen to us?"

No sooner had the words left his mouth than the deli door flew open, and out stormed an old man — short, round-faced, with an incredible paunch hidden behind a greasy white apron. His stomach formed a little shelf in front of him. It would have been a great place to put a bowling trophy, but somehow I doubted he had one.

He shook a two-pronged meat fork at us. "Are you crazy, Mr. Cardone, bringing the police to my building?" His many chins bobbed as he spoke and, below them, the apron jiggled. "Police bring health inspectors, and building inspectors, and before you know it — hassles!"

"How do you know my name?" I asked. It took a few seconds to sink in that this was Plotnick, our new landlord.

"Because you look just exactly like the other Mr. Cardone, without the muscles."

Joe and I look absolutely nothing alike. "Well, I'm sorry, Mr. Plotnick, but we had no choice. My brother's car's been stolen."

The landlord shrugged. "What's one little car compared to the health of a real person? I'm an old man. It could be on your conscience that I have a heart attack."

"You should consider a low cholesterol diet," said Ferguson seriously.

Plotnick looked daggers at him. "Who is this person?"

I introduced Ferguson and Don. "They're houseguests." Plotnick looked suspicious. "They're staying with me for — for a little while."

"How little?"

"We don't know yet."

Plotnick's eyes narrowed. "Okay, Mr. Cardone, but you should remember — apartment 2C is a one-person apartment. In a one-person apartment lives one person. If three persons live there, it isn't a one-person apartment anymore."

"One more thing," I remembered. "One of the stairs was weak, and Don kind of fell through when we were — "

"What?" Plotnick reached up to tear at his hair, but he didn't have any, so he clutched at the air just above his head. He glared at Don. "You broke my stairs?"

"The wood was all rotted out, and I guess my foot went right through."

"Vandalism!" cried Plotnick. "Mr. Cardone, I'm afraid I'll have to ask your brother to terminate his lease."

I was horrified. "Terminate it? Why?"

"He has brought an undesirable element to this neighborhood," Plotnick said haughtily.

"Actually, Mr. Plotnick," the Peach put in, "I don't follow your line of reasoning. The hole in the stairs comes not from Don, but from your negligent upkeep."

"There's something annoying about you, Mr. Peach," said Plotnick. "Could it be the fact that you have a big mouth? You accuse me of not taking care of my building? Me? Plotnick, a respected member of this community? I ask you, is it my fault this big dummy goes stomping down my stairs like a wild man?"

"What if we agree to pay for the repairs?" I said

25

suddenly. I knew the hole in the staircase wasn't our fault. But if Joe came home and found his lease terminated, the three of us wouldn't be too far behind it.

"I'll give you the bill," said Plotnick pleasantly. "Welcome to my building." And he walked back into the deli without another word.

Three

We went to the supermarket and bought instant everything. Instant macaroni and cheese, instant rice, instant potatoes, instant pasta, frozen vegetables, precooked chicken, and an assortment of TV dinners. It was the instant hash browns Don set fire to as we were getting ready for our first day of work the next morning. I was still in the shower when I heard Plotnick's distant voice through the ventilation duct yelling,

"Put it out, Mr. Cardone! Smother it! Put water on it! Don't burn down my building!"

Wrapping myself in a towel, I ran out to find the apartment thick with black smoke. Ferguson and

Don were standing there staring at a flaming fry-pan.

I threw open the sole window in the bathroom, which did little to clear away the smoke. Then I put my face right up to the ventilation duct and bellowed as loud as I could, *"No problem! Just a little accident cooking breakfast! Everything's under control!"*

"I'm not deaf, Mr. Cardone," came Plotnick's reply. "Come down to my restaurant. I'll make for you a breakfast."

By this time, the fire was out, but thick clouds of dense smoke were billowing from the burnt pan.

"You have to use low heat," the Peach was lecturing, "especially with this type of pan — "

"I give up." Don threw his hands in the air. "I'm sorry I didn't take the Peachfuzz course on how to do everything in the known universe. I'm a moron."

"Not a moron," said Ferguson. "Just a pyro-maniac."

"Hey." I stepped between them. "Plotnick's got breakfast on for us in the deli."

The inside of the Olympiad Delicatessen was almost, but not quite, cozy. It was also almost, but not quite, clean, and almost, but not quite, comfortable. Plotnick was the nerve center, cooking and delivering steaming plates of almost, but not quite, food to a handful of customers scattered throughout the deli's booths and tables. He presided over the counter like a king over his court, brandishing the lethal meat fork, his royal scepter.

He waved us over to the corner booth, where

three glasses of orange juice and three steaming cups of coffee waited. "Good morning, Mr. Ferguson Peach, who is just only a houseguest and not really living in my building," he said sarcastically, tossing an envelope in front of Ferguson. "So how come today you got a letter sent right here?"

I looked at the return address and then the postmark. The Peach's mother, anticipating her precious child getting homesick early, had mailed the letter three days before we'd even left Owen Sound. Don looked completely disgusted.

Ferguson was unperturbed. "I told my mother where to reach me," he explained blandly.

"What are you — a brain surgeon that you should be available twenty-four hours a day? Maybe I should change my restaurant to Olympiad Delicatessen and Message Center, just in case the President of the United States needs to talk to you while you're just only a houseguest who's not really living in my building."

"The President probably won't call," said the Peach, turning his attention to his juice.

With a haughty snort, Plotnick took our orders and came back five minutes later with three plates of scrambled eggs. The food may not have set us up for the whole day, but it sure lubricated our chassis. Plotnick's idea of breakfast was grease smothered in grease. Afterward, we settled back to let it all ooze down.

"This place is great," sighed Don, interrupting Ferguson's cholesterol count. "This is the real world — good old-fashioned food in a down-to-earth restaurant while you're living on your own, and you're heading out to a day's work for a day's pay."

I nodded enthusiastically. What's a little grease when you're having the summer of your life?

"We'll probably be regulars here," Don continued, "and this will be considered 'our booth,' and no one else will sit here, and — "

"Hey, Mr. Champion," piped Plotnick from the counter. "Get out of 'your booth' and come and pay 'your bill.' "

We paid up. Behind the cash register stood an old mesh playpen, full to the brim with an assortment of hubcaps, each with its own price tag. My eyes met Ferguson's, and we both shrugged at the same time. That was weird. Salami, yes. But hubcaps? Where did they fit in?

No sooner did the thought cross my mind than there was a screech of tires, and Plotnick stiffened like a pointer. We all watched as a dark sedan shot up Bathurst Street at top speed. Right before Pitt, a huge pothole yawned in its path. An enormous clang rocked the neighborhood, and suddenly a shiny, spinning hubcap was airborne. In a single motion, Plotnick reached under the counter, produced a butterfly net, and was out the door. He threw himself heroically in the path of the hurtling cap, and netted it with a delicate flick of the wrist. We joined in the applause.

Flushed with triumph, Plotnick waddled back into the deli, rushed to the griddle to flip a pancake, and stopped to examine his prize. "Very good condition," he said with satisfaction; he slapped on a sticker that read $19.95, and tossed the hubcap into the playpen with the rest.

Rush hour in the city: We saw more cars than pass through Owen Sound in fifty years. They were all right in front of our streetcar and then, after we transferred, in front of our bus. At a quarter to nine, still sitting amidst the honking of horns and the cursing of drivers, we abandoned the bus and sprinted the remaining twelve blocks to Plastics Unlimited.

The factory was a thing of beauty, and I know this because Ferguson couldn't think of a single thing wrong with it. It was a sprawling chrome complex in an area of light industry, and somehow it looked like success. I was really impressed when Don's uncle's personal file clerk led us on a tour of the manufacturing plant. Plastics Unlimited was gearing up to fill an order for 800,000 of those wands with the rings on the end that little kids dip in soapy water and blow bubbles with.

Finally the tour was over, and we were led into the plush outer office, and through the heavy oak door marked *Harold P. Robb, President.*

Don's uncle looked like a taller, older version of Don. But apparently he didn't notice the resemblance, because he leaped out of his padded leather chair, and enfolded Ferguson Peach in a massive bear hug.

"Donny!" he bellowed jovially. "I'd know you anywhere! You look just like your mother!"

"No, no, Uncle Harry!" said Don in consternation. "Over here! *I'm* Don!"

"Right — uh, right." Without embarrassment, he transferred his hug to the correct nephew. "Yes, I see now. Just like Miriam, my favorite sister."

"My mother is Anne," Don reminded his uncle.

"She's great, too," said Mr. Robb, unfazed. "Too bad she moved to that little dumpy town up north somewhere. Now let me see — what was the name of that place?"

"Owen Sound," said Don.

"Yeah. How did you know?"

Don was getting impatient. "I moved with her. I'm her son."

His uncle was thunderstruck. "Miriam lives in Owen Sound, too? Boy, we sure do lose touch. Well now — welcome to Plastics Unlimited. You three are going to be feeders. I want you to know that's a tremendous responsibility."

I couldn't contain my excitement. "What do we do?"

"You feed a sheet of plastic into the stamping machine, which cuts out twenty-four bubble wands and sends them on the conveyor belt to packaging."

"And then?" asked Don.

"And then you feed another sheet," his uncle replied.

"That's it?"

"That's it," he said cheerfully. "Until coffee break. Then until lunch. Then until five."

I felt my eyes glazing over. A guy who didn't speak English escorted us to our places in a huge assembly line, issued us safety glasses, wished us what sounded like, "Fuffle leffer thuffs," and left us to our fate.

About eight thousand bubble wands later, I dared to look up and glance over at Ferguson. He had already run out of plastic sheets and, while awaiting a new supply, was gazing around with rapt interest. Now, that was always a danger sign. When the Peach started thinking about something, chances were he was redesigning, fixing, and improving in his mind.

Don noticed this, too, and at coffee break made his opinion clear. "Look, Peachfuzz, if you stick your nose into everybody's business and get yourself fired, don't expect Jason and me to support you."

"I haven't said a word," said Ferguson blandly. "I'm too involved in this fascinating job."

Don flushed red. "You think you're too good to work on an assembly line? During World War II, what made this country strong? Our production lines, that's what!"

Ferguson nodded sagely. "I guess World War III is going to be fought with bubble wands. What are we going to use for ammo — atomic soap?"

I had to step in. "Cut it out, you guys. There's nothing wrong with our jobs. Everybody has to start at the bottom."

At that point, the foreman stood up and bellowed, "Flangel dipla noof-spif!" and about sixty people went back to work, so we went, too.

It happened less than an hour before quitting time. I was carrying my bin of plastic cuttings to the recycling station when I noticed that Ferguson had left his machine. I spotted him seated at the production computer, explaining something to two fascinated engineers.

"I'll kill him!" hissed Don behind me.

"You'll have to get in line!" I was feeling pretty homicidal myself. Here we were, first day on the job, dying to make a good impression, and there was Ferguson, goofing off, playing with a computer. We both stood there, signaling at the oblivious Ferguson, until the foreman ordered us back to work. At least, I think he did. I had developed the theory that "noof-spif" meant "work." What *language* was that?

All the way home, we gave it to Ferguson. As usual, the Peach was totally calm.

"I didn't desert my machine," he explained, hanging on by two fingers to a leather strap while our packed bus sat in traffic. "The chief engineer was having a temper tantrum, and he yelled that he couldn't understand why no one in the company was familiar with the Magnetronic 500 series computer. So I told him the truth. I know all about it."

"You were supposed to mind your own business," growled Don. "Make sure it doesn't happen again."

"Don't worry about that," said Ferguson. "The design software is all de-bugged now. Tomorrow I can go back to the business of making bubble wands, for in a world without bubble wands, I do not wish to live."

Score another one for the Peach. Don seethed the rest of the way home.

Bubble wands became as much a part of our world as breathing, eating, sleeping, and calling the police to ask about Joe's car. As the week went by and the numbers mounted up towards that magic tally of 800,000, I started having dreams about traveling through the universe, trapped inside a giant bubble, blown by colossal lips through the great-granddaddy of all bubble wands.

Don, too, was having bubble trouble in his dreams, and woke up each morning with the taste of soap in his mouth.

Each day we spent our commuting time counting up all the bubble sets we'd owned in grade school. We'd been so young we'd thought they'd grown on trees or something, not that some poor sap had to stand there all day, feeding dumb sheets of plastic into a dumb machine.

I suppose I don't have to mention the interest factor, which was approximately zero. In fact, the only thing that kept us from lapsing into a coma on the job was the noise. The stamping machine made a crashing sound that would jar your back teeth loose. One night I caught Ferguson, crouched over Don's sleeping form on the couch, yelling, *"Ka-chunk! Ka-chunk!"* into his ear. The Peach dove back into his bed just as Don awoke with a start, scared that he'd fallen asleep at his machine. The Peach was like that sometimes.

Impressions of my first job: When I pick my real career, it's going to be something quiet, like florist, or mortician.

Ferguson had none of these problems. As the week progressed, he spent less and less time making bubble wands. When we arrived at the plant on Tuesday morning, four engineers and two computer programmers were crowded around the Peach's machine, waiting for him. He was whisked

35

off to the production computer for a consultation that lasted until noon.

Back at his machine after lunch, the Peach barely had the chance to make a few hundred bubble wands before two men from the executive offices came and spoke at length with the chief engineer. In no time at all, Ferguson stuck his nose into that, too, and soon he was typing away at the computer, as the execs were laughing, applauding, and patting him on the back.

Don was furious. "You know what's going to happen when they count his production and see how many wands he *didn't* make today? He's putting all our jobs in jeopardy!"

I was looking in perplexity at the production computer. "He certainly seems to be getting along well with all the muckamucks."

"Sure. He's goofing off, making friends, while we work our butts off. It can only end one way. He's going to get canned."

I shrugged. "Well, if he does, he'll just have to find another job. He can't expect us to support him all summer."

Don jammed a sheet savagely into the stamper. "I'm not feeding him. Peachfuzz starves. The world will be better off."

I smiled in spite of myself. "Come on."

"It'll be a national holiday," Don insisted, his eyes growing dreamy. " 'No More Peachfuzz Day.' I can see it now — a big parade, with little children carrying peach pits. And after the mayor's speech, they all chant, 'Nothing needs fixing! It's all okay!' Then they throw their peach pits down the sewer."

We both laughed. We feeders get a little crazy

sometimes. It comes from all the responsibility. It's one of those big stress jobs.

It was amazing how quickly 1 Pitt Street became home. We fell into a routine: breakfast at the Olympiad, brown bag lunches, various snacks at home, and dinner out. That gave us a chance to explore a different part of the city every night, and soon we knew the bus and subway routes as though we'd been here all our lives.

Ours was a quiet building, if you didn't count Plotnick and his big mouth. Our contact with the neighbors was generally nothing more than a polite smile or wave, and a murmured "Good morning." We never even got to know their names, as the apartment doors were unmarked, and the landlord took in the mail and handed it out himself, since there were no individual boxes. So we developed our own secret nicknames for our fellow tenants.

Apartment 2A, right across the hall, housed the Stripper, a six-foot-tall lady with a fabulous figure. We figured she'd started out as a dewy-eyed starlet, but now, pushing forty from the wrong side, she was the makeup company's best customer. Plotnick tried to convince us what a high-class building he ran by telling us she was an artistic dancer. But Don saw through this.

"A dancer just dances," he explained. "An artistic dancer dances without clothes. The more artistic, the less clothes."

Next to 2A was 2B, the love nest of Romeo and Juliet. They were a middle-aged couple who went to work every morning, took their meals in the deli, and spent all the rest of their time kissing.

37

2C was us, and our next door neighbor in 2D was the Phantom. We never saw the Phantom, since he never left the apartment. But he was Plotnick's favorite tenant, because he always paid the rent on time.

"He didn't make me one hassle," said the landlord fondly. He glared at Ferguson and Don. "And he never has houseguests."

The weird part was, for a guy who stayed cooped up inside his apartment, the Phantom seemed to have a vast acquaintance. He was on the phone with friends all day and half the night. We envisioned apartments all over town, with other Phantoms, all having elaborate social lives without ever stepping out the door.

The stairway up to the third floor was the steepest, narrowest, darkest, and most treacherous climb this side of Everest. Up this cliff, several times a day, ascended a tiny, frail, silver-haired lady who looked about two hundred years old. We called her God's Grandmother.

God's Grandmother was the friendliest person in the building, and had a smile for everyone, even Plotnick. She must have been in better shape than she looked, because she jogged several times each day. It was torture to watch. She fluttered along the sidewalk like a leaf in the wind, and every step seemed like it would be her last.

Another denizen of the third floor was the Ugly Man, who really wasn't all that ugly, except that he had only one thick, black, bushy eyebrow, which stretched all the way across his forehead. His beady little eyes peered out from under it like a rodent hiding in a hedge. He was the least congenial tenant, and always seemed to be muttering obscenities under his breath. My mother couldn't have washed his mouth out with soap. She'd have had to go for the Drano.

Maybe the Ugly Man was in this lousy mood because he was in love with another neighbor, Wayne Gretzky's Sister. We named her that because she looked exactly — I mean *exactly* — like a female version of Don's hero, Wayne Gretzky. We didn't see much of her but, when we did, she was usually studiously ignoring the Ugly Man.

That left the quietest tenant of 1 Pitt Street, a man we called the Assassin. He was kind of a mystery — a guy in a crummy third floor walk-up, who wore fifteen-hundred-dollar suits and Gucci loafers. He had a waxed mustache, and the coldest eyes you've ever seen. He came and went at odd hours, and always carried a thin black attaché case — perfect size for a machine gun. Even when we found out he was a librarian, we kept up his nickname. He looked like Death, swift and professional.

Last, but not least, came Plotnick himself, who lived in a large apartment on the first floor behind the deli. If nothing else, our landlord was fair. He was no nastier to us than to the rest of his tenants and deli customers.

We fit right in. The Stripper, Romeo and Juliet, the Phantom, God's Grandmother, the Ugly Man, Wayne Gretzky's Sister, the Assassin, and the Three Stooges.

And as I drifted off to sleep listening to the Phantom on the phone, planning the menu for a party he would *never* attend, I reflected that the Dream Summer was shaping up pretty well. If we could get the car back, and if Don and I could just keep Ferguson out of trouble at work, everything would be fine.

Four

On Wednesday, Ferguson Peach's lack of productivity at Plastics Unlimited came to the attention of the foreman. At least, we think it did. He stood in front of the Peach at coffee break and gave him a long lecture about "noof-spif," which we were pretty sure meant "work."

"You see?" Don challenged after the foreman had moved on to fuffle at somebody else. "If you don't smarten up and do some work, you're out of here."

"You look after your noof-spif," said Ferguson, "and I'll look after mine."

"You aren't doing any noof-spif!" wailed Don.

But Ferguson was on his way to the production

computer, where the engineers waited, checking their watches and wringing their hands.

On Thursday, Ferguson didn't make any bubble wands at all. Instead, he held court at the computer, typing furiously, stopping only to make rough sketches on paper.

"That's it!" seethed Don. "No more Mr. Nice Guy! As soon as he gets back here, *he* goes into the stamping machine! Some poor kid's going to get a Peachfuzz bubble wand — which'll keep telling him how to blow better bubbles!"

But Ferguson did not return. Instead, more and more people gathered at the computer to see what was going on. By coffee break, the entire engineering staff was there, and the excited babble was drowning out the stamping machines. As the morning wore on, executives trickled one by one from the offices to crowd around Ferguson until, finally, Don's Uncle Harry, president of the whole company, came to investigate the goings-on.

Don was turning purple.

All eyes were on the screen as Ferguson deftly pounded the keyboard. Then he got up and pointed to several places around the plant. After that, the whole crowd of thirty-plus people disappeared into the executive offices, taking the Peach with them.

Three hours later, we were summoned to see Don's uncle. Don had a plan. "I'm going to save our jobs at all costs, Jason, so don't try to stop me. When my uncle asks what's the story here, I'm going to nail Peachfuzz to the wall. I'll say we hardly even know the idiot, and that we only need him for the rent. Then I'll apologize like crazy, and maybe we'll get through this one alive."

I was really confused. *Was* Ferguson about to be fired? All I could think of was my summer. Could Ferguson get another job, or would he be on the train back to Owen Sound tomorrow? Could Don and I cover the rent on just two salaries? Or would we be back on the train after Ferguson's, to be greeted by my father and his four favorite words — I, *told*, *you*, and *so*? I gritted my teeth. If that happened, there really would be a "No More Peachfuzz Day." I, Jason Cardone, would throw out the first peach pit.

"Donny, where did you find this guy?" Uncle Harry was referring to Ferguson, who was seated in a big leather chair while we stood.

I could see the wheels turning in Don's head. But when he opened his mouth, only panic poured out. "He's nobody! I never met him before in my life! He's an idiot! Just some guy off the street! I'm not responsible! Don't blame me!"

Harold Robb just stared at his nephew. "An idiot? Why, Fergie is the most remarkable young man it's ever been my pleasure to meet. I can't thank you enough for bringing him to me."

Don goggled. "You're welcome."

The president got up and put his hand on the Peach's shoulder. "He's a genius! He's going to save this company millions! In all my years in business, I've never met such a gifted individual. Do you know that he can take a look at an operation, and immediately see ways to improve it?"

No kidding. Don and I exchanged glances. The Peach's expression didn't alter.

"Which is what I've brought you in here to discuss. Part of Fergie's complete plant overhaul involves an automatic feeding system, so Plastics Unlimited doesn't need feeders anymore."

It took a second or two for this to sink in.

"We're fired?" I barely whispered.

Don was stunned into silence.

"Of course not," said Uncle Harry. "Can't run the place without my boy Fergie. But you two — well, that's business, right? Tomorrow's your last day."

"But — but you're my uncle!" gasped Don.

"All the more reason why you don't want any special treatment," beamed our ex-employer. "A man's got to make his own way in this world. Just look at Ferguson here. What a mind! What a *mind*!"

Don was begging now. "Couldn't we be transferred to another section?"

"Sorry, we're fully staffed. And you have the least seniority, so you have to go."

"But I'm *family*!" Don whined.

"Nepotism has no place in business," his uncle replied. "This is a tough world, Donny. Think of how fortunate you are to learn all about it at your age."

The end.

Ferguson was invited to stay and have dinner with the executives, and Don and I went home. By unspoken agreement, we jammed all the Peach's clothes into his suitcase, zipped it up, and threw it out the window. Then we turned out all the lights and cranked the stereo up to 9.

At eight-thirty, Ferguson showed up, good-natured as ever, suitcase in hand. We had no words; we just stared grim death at him.

He said, "Sorry," and began to unpack.

I blew up. "Sorry? *Sorry?* We're obsolete, thanks to you! Now what are we supposed to do — go down to the museum and stand in a glass case marked *Feeders. Late Twentieth Century?*"

The Peach just shrugged.

Don went for his throat, and I had to leap between them. "The important thing," I said, straining to hold them apart, "is that we can't let our parents find out we've been fired. Remember, the jobs were the number-one condition for this trip."

"Right!" exclaimed Don. He shook his fist at Ferguson. "If you slip up in one of your hourly letters to Mommy, and mention us getting canned, our folks'll freak out and drag us back home."

"I'll take it under advisement," murmured the Peach.

But I knew Ferguson wouldn't tell. And Don's uncle was no risk — he couldn't even remember which of his sisters was Don's mother. Absolutely nobody could know we'd lost our jobs.

When we went down to the deli for breakfast the next morning, we found *The Toronto Star* Employment section spread out on the table of our booth.

I looked over at Plotnick, who was behind the counter, involved in a hubcap sale. "What's this for?" I called.

The landlord looked up. "Just in case you should happen to know two persons looking for employment as of today."

"Yeah, well, we don't know anyone," I snapped. Was Plotnick psychic or something?

Plotnick handed the hubcap customer his change. "Okay, Mr. Cardone, but just remember, the first of the month is coming this weekend. And jobs for feeders are hard to come by with all the mechanization these days."

I spied the ventilation duct grating right behind Plotnick's head. "Mr. Plotnick, have you been listening in on us?"

The landlord brandished his meat fork defensively. "It's my fault you gentlemen are yelling and screaming all the time? You want privacy? Try talking like a normal person." He waddled over to our booth, and I tried to picture him trussed up like a roast pig, with an apple in his mouth. "Okay, what'll it be? Mr. Peach, you first, since you're paying the bills from now on. And by the way, congratulations on your promotion."

Don was in a nasty mood. "When are you going to fix that stair? I almost killed myself this morning!"

"Look who's talking," said Plotnick righteously. "I asked you to come smash up my building? Watch where you're going!" He turned to Ferguson. "So, Mr. Peach — how much money do you make?"

I slammed my hand down on the tabletop. "Mr. Plotnick, you don't ask a guy something like that!"

The landlord shrugged. "A person is interested. Six figures maybe?"

The Peach laughed. "They bumped me up fifty bucks a week."

Plotnick was insulted on Ferguson's behalf. "If

you hold yourself cheap, Mr. Peach, you get treated like a bargain.''

"I'm not exactly a career man," Ferguson pointed out. "I'm only going to be there for a couple of months."

"All the more reason why you should grab fast!" said Donald Trump in a greasy apron. "You let me talk to your thief of a boss, and soon you'll be on Easy Street. I only charge twenty percent."

"No, thank you."

"But you'll be rich! You'll live in a penthouse!"

I pictured the third floor. "Why? Is the Ugly Man moving out?"

Plotnick ignored my wisecrack. "Don't think only of yourself, Mr. Peach. Remember, you've got two unemployed bums to support."

I looked over at the other bum. We'd have to find work — and fast!

At Plastics Unlimited, Ferguson got paid, and Don and I got paid off. We stopped at the bank on Bathurst and put most of the money into a checking account on our three signatures. Our convenience cards would be sent in the mail, but the teller presented us with a checkbook on the spot. None of us had ever written checks before. We were psyched.

As we left the bank, Don couldn't take his eyes off our passbook. "We've got over a thousand dollars." He grinned. "A thou. A grand."

"The rent's coming up tomorrow," the Peach pointed out.

"Six hundred and eighty-five bucks," Don shrugged. "We're rich. Let's celebrate."

47

Before we knew it, he'd hailed a taxi, and we were headed against the traffic downtown.

"Where are we going?" I asked.

"Tonight is the first night of the rest of our lives as swinging city guys!" declared Mr. Wonderful grandly.

"Well — uh — I was thinking of checking to see if there was any word on the car — "

"You need to forget the car for one night," advised Don. "We're going to drown ourselves in loud music, colored lights, and hot babes."

Ferguson laughed in his face. "Babes?"

"Shut up, Peachfuzz," snapped Don. "What do you know about women — besides the fact that they all agree what a geek you are? Come on. It's Friday night! Let's get some action. Jason, how long's it been since you broke up with old what's-her-face?"

I reddened. Amy Loezer, my one and only girl-friend, had ditched me in February. That was just after she made me throw away my *Sports Illustrated* swimsuit issue because it exploited women. One day I opened her locker, and there was my brother Joe, his muscles oiled, smiling out at me, Mr. February. There was even a lipstick smear on Joe's bulging bicep. I tore it into a billion pieces, and she never spoke to me again.

"What about you?" I countered. "What was the logic behind you dumping Teresa last month?" Teresa is Don's ex. She's going to have trouble deciding whether to be a high-fashion model or a nuclear physicist.

But Don just smiled. "That was a masterstroke. A perfect move."

"How do you figure that? It doesn't make sense."

"That's the whole point," Mr. Wonderful argued smugly. "There was no reason to end it with Teresa, so when I did, what did everybody think?"

"That you're stupid?" suggested Ferguson innocently.

"That I've got something going for me even beyond what everybody sees. So I've kind of *traded* Teresa for future considerations — and in September I'll have my pick of any chick I want all year."

"But you lost Teresa when you still like her," I protested.

Don shrugged. "Let's concentrate on tonight. Now, what's the key to hooking up with a chick?"

I wasn't prepared for a quiz. "Uh — I guess if she thinks you're a nice person — "

"No, no, no," interrupted Don in exasperation. "Girls say they want nice guys, but they never do."

The cab stopped in front of a giant neon sign that blazed:

CLUB MOONTRIX — TORONTO'S PREMIER TEEN CLUB

"The first impression is the most important thing," whispered Don as we paid our admission. "So watch what you do, how you walk, what you say. Take medium-sized steps, and try not to smile so much. It's better if you look like you're p.o.-ed about something. Not too much. Just a little."

Club Moontrix was huge — bigger than the entire Plastics Unlimited plant area. The dancing hadn't started yet because they were still serving dinner. We got a table and ordered three burgers.

The Peach and I wanted pizza, but Mr. Wonderful insisted it would do too much damage to our breath.

"As soon as a girl steps into a place like this," he told us as we sipped on our Cokes, "she divides all the guys into the nimrods and the cool people. You haven't even said 'Hi' to her yet, and it could be all over if you're in the wrong category."

Ferguson signaled the waitress. "Excuse me, do you know if these napkins are made of recycled paper?"

Don held his head. "If you look up nimrod in the dictionary, there's probably a picture of Peach-fuzz."

As we were eating, the place was steadily filling up. By the time the music started, it was wall-to-wall people. The beat was bone-jarring, and colored lights and lasers electrified the dance floor. If they moved a great place like this to Owen Sound, it would probably be shut down by the police. For this kind of excitement, you couldn't beat downtown Toronto. We just stood there for a long time, soaking up the atmosphere, and then Don said it was time to mingle with the ladies — "catch a rap," as he put it.

But we didn't. Instead, we walked around the club while Don looked at every girl in the place — and I mean *every* girl. It was like he was shopping for a house. He would walk ten feet, stop, check out the scene, walk ten feet, stop, check out the scene. We must have circled the club five times that way. After about an hour, Ferguson gave up and went to the bathroom to read a book. I was dying to ask somebody to dance, but Don said no.

"Just watch. And take notes."

Who was I to argue with the guy who dumped Teresa Barstow? Finally, after all that walking and staring, he headed over to the soda bar.

"I guess it's not our night — " I began sympathetically.

"Are you crazy?" he gasped. "I can't miss!" He ordered the Moontrix Mountain, the most expensive drink in the place, a giant whipped-cream-topped milkshake float that would fill a toilet bowl. Then he stuck two straws into the concoction and went off to share it with — who?

You had to give Don credit. After carefully scouting out every human female in the building, when he went after his quarry, it looked totally spontaneous — guy sees girl, guy offers drink. He didn't even say a word. He just pushed a straw in her direction and grinned an invitation.

You saw it coming, but you couldn't stop it — two thirsty people and a Moontrix Mountain. She lunged at her straw, and Don lunged at his. There was a crack as loud as a gunshot as forehead met forehead. Don staggered back, but the girl crumpled to the floor, unconscious. The entire Moontrix Mountain slipped out of his hand and plopped down right on her head.

There was a lot of screaming and scrambling, and suddenly Mr. Wonderful was at my elbow. "I think we'd better get out of here," he said. "I just killed that girl."

"You can't leave now!" I raged. "She's out cold!"

Don rubbed his brow. "But when she wakes up, she's going to be *mad*!"

I grabbed him and started dragging him into the fray. "We have to find out if she's okay."

We pushed through the crowd of spectators to where the victim lay. Guess who was at the center of everything, directing traffic, barking orders, and applying wet towelettes to the girl's forehead? Ferguson Peach.

Pretty soon she was on her feet again, although dripping with Moontrix Mountain. She cleaned up a little, and we hustled her out for some air. Even after that vicious coco-bump and a drenching with a giant drink, you could tell she was great-looking. She was tall and slim, with a really natural look to her. She didn't put on makeup with a trowel like the Stripper. Also, it didn't hurt that she was wearing a miniskirt, revealing fantastic legs.

We introduced ourselves, and she told us her name was Jessica Lincoln. I booted Don in the back of the leg and looked at him sternly.

"Uh — yeah," he said, studying his shoes like a four-year-old admitting he'd thrown his Tonka truck through a picture window. "I'm sorry about — you know. It was an accident."

"Don't worry about it," she said. "I left myself open."

"Open?" queried the Peach.

"In my *tae kwan do* class, they teach us always to expect an attack, no matter how safe you think you may be."

"So you're into martial arts?" I jumped in quickly. If we ran out of conversation, she might *leave*, and I didn't have her phone number yet.

"Only as self-defense," said Jessica. "There are

all kinds of criminals and lunatics on the streets of this city. I don't want to become a statistic."

"Have you ever been mugged?" I asked.

"That's what scares me," she admitted. "I've lived in Toronto my whole life and I've never had the slightest problem."

"That's good," I said. Wasn't it?

"It means my number could be coming up any minute!" she reasoned. "The law of averages is against me."

"Actually," the Peach began, "according to probability theory — "

"What good is probability theory when some drug-crazed maniac is ripping off your watch?" she interrupted.

"We've had kind of an incident," I said, almost proudly. "My brother's car was stolen."

Jessica looked triumphant. "Society is one big smelly cesspool. You want to go out somewhere?"

My head snapped to attention. I'd been contemplating the cesspool when she threw out this curve. She was looking straight at Don. No question who she was asking.

Suddenly Mr. Wonderful was alive in the conversation. In ten seconds, he had a taxi. Don, who had been ready to leave Jessica unconscious in a pool of melting milkshake, got the girl. I got "it was very nice meeting you." I hated both their guts.

"Hold it," said Jessica as Don was about to climb into the cab beside her. "What do you think you're doing?"

Don was mystified. "Going with you."

"Not like that you're not."

Don surveyed himself in anxiety. Could it be that there was a flaw in the outfit he'd spent hours selecting?

"Your wallet's in your back pocket!" exclaimed Jessica. "Do you want to make yourself a target for a pickpocket?"

"No way!" agreed Don. This was the guy who refused to carry anything in his front pocket because it threw off the visual symmetry of his lower body. Not only did he move his wallet, but Ferguson and I had to move ours, too.

I stood fuming as they drove off. "I can't believe it! Why would she go with *him*?"

Ferguson shrugged. "Maybe society *is* a smelly cesspool."

"Don was right about one thing," I seethed. "Girls really don't want nice guys. If it wasn't for us, she'd still be out cold, wearing dessert. *He* was ready to head for Switzerland. And what do we get? Anti-pickpocket advice!" I pulled out my wallet and jammed it into its former position. "Hey, pickpockets, lookee here! It's party time!"

The Peach put a sympathetic arm around my shoulder. "At least we know he's safe from crime. I pity the poor sap who tries to mug *her*."

Since July 1st was Canada Day, and Plotnick refused to do business on a holiday, our rent was due the next morning. I broke in our new checkbook — number 001, to Plotnick, $685. Writing checks makes a guy feel very independent. It almost made me forget my telephone call from my parents, who made boring small talk for twenty minutes, leaving long pauses so I could break down and beg them to come and take me home. I filled in this dead air by raving about Plastics Unlimited, telling them everything about the company except the fact that Don and I didn't work there anymore.

Don was still bragging about his enchanting evening with Jessica Lincoln. "I was 'on' last night, and Jessica knew it. I was the perfect combination of hipness and coolness. You want to know the best part? She lives right near here, just up Bathurst. Convenient or what?"

"Great," I mumbled, without enthusiasm.

Don didn't get the message. "I could tell she was really impressed when I bought her a single perfect rose from this vendor on the street."

"She must have been devastated," put in Ferguson. "She had her heart set on a bullet-proof vest."

"Shut up, Peachfuzz," Don said mildly. Last night had put him in a mellow mood, and not even the Peach could rile him. "You're just jealous. We've got to work on scaring up a woman for you." He looked thoughtful. "There must be some boring people around. Maybe a lady professor of Stonehenge."

I was determined not to show it, but my guts were churning. If Mr. Wonderful said one more word, I was going to pop him. Obviously Jessica had no taste at all. Any idiot could see that I would treat her like a queen, and Don would treat her like a customer at the ice cream parlor — take a number and wait — "Now serving number twenty-three."

I tore out the rent check. "Let's go pay up."

With the walk to the deli came a pleasant surprise. Plotnick had finally gotten around to having the stair fixed. In fact, he'd had all the stairs fixed, and a new bannister installed. And carpeting.

God's Grandmother was flitting up and down barefoot, enjoying the new luxury. "Isn't it lovely?"

"Yes, ma'am," I agreed. "I never expected Mr. Plotnick to do all this."

The bill came to $319. Plotnick handed it to me, skewered on the end of his meat fork.

"Wow," I said. "How much do we owe you?"

"You're maybe having trouble with your eyesight, Mr. Cardone? It says $319."

"Yeah, but that's for the whole job," I protested. "What's our portion?"

Plotnick was patient. "A staircase is like a chain, Mr. Cardone. If one of the links is broken, the whole chain is *kaput*."

"Then," put in Ferguson, "fixing one link would save the whole chain."

"Better to get a new chain," said Plotnick evenly. "And that costs $319."

I could feel my face flaming. "I won't pay!"

Plotnick shrugged. "That's your privilege. And just to show you I'm a reasonable man, I'll hold off my eviction proceedings so your brother can be present in court."

In Owen Sound, people like Plotnick go to jail. But in Toronto, here he was, holding all the cards. I remembered my brother's message: *Whatever you do, DON'T lose me this lease.* Whatever you do. Even if you have to hand over three hundred bucks to this hoodlum in a greasy apron.

"But it was only one stair," I managed weakly.

Plotnick nodded sympathetically. "Prices these days. Out of sight. Your brother, also Mr. Cardone, used to say that a lot. Nice boy. Big muscles. I'd miss him if he moved away."

I'll say this about Plotnick. He certainly knew how to get to the heart of the matter. I looked at Ferguson and Don, who nodded. I wrote him another check, number 002, and felt even more independent — like I was alone on a desert island surrounded by crocodiles.

With two of us unemployed, and Ferguson's next paycheck six and a half long days away, we were left with exactly $17.60 to live on — $5.86 per person for next week.

JULY

Five

Living for a week on seventeen bucks was a special talent. Fortunately we still had some groceries left — nothing fancy — soup, sandwiches, Kraft Dinner, and cereal for breakfast. A care package of bran muffins from Mrs. Peach arrived by mail, and we were really thrilled until we found out that Ferguson's mom bakes hockey pucks. It was agreed, even by the Peach, that only after going through the garbage would we resort to the muffins.

Every penny counted. We had enough cash to send Ferguson on the bus to and from stupid Plastics Unlimited, but if Don or I got jobs out of the neighborhood, we would have to walk. As for entertainment — forget it.

We were still stinging from the big ripoff, especially Don. Things always went perfectly for Mr. Wonderful, so he had no experience in dealing with anything less than sunshine and roses. He seemed more bewildered than upset. Plotnick had overloaded his brain.

"I still don't see how he can get away with it!" Don seethed. "Surely there must be some board of review or something that we can complain to!"

"I'm sure there is," I said. "We'd probably win, too. But by the time all the technicalities got straightened out, it would be months — maybe years! And Joe would be back from Europe, kicked out of his apartment, and we'd be wrapped in plastic, sitting in the supermarket with the rest of the hamburger!"

"Well, maybe," said Don. "But it stinks. I mean — things aren't supposed to go this way."

It didn't make us feel any better when an envelope arrived from my brother in England. Inside was a snapshot of Joe, carrying a gorgeous blonde through the surf. On the back was scribbled: *Me and Daphne at Brighton. P.S. I forgot to warn you. If you break something in Plotnick's building, don't tell him, or he'll fix up the whole place and try to make you pay for it.*

We cursed the mail. Why couldn't these words of wisdom have gotten here three hundred and nineteen bucks ago?

On Monday morning, I was taking a shower, trying to conserve soap when, through the shower curtain, I thought I spotted movement out on the fire escape. Shocked, I turned off the water, wrapped myself in a towel, and jumped out of the tub. I watched in horror as the air conditioner was lifted out of the window, and a hairy arm, big as a tree trunk, reached in and flipped the lock.

My mind screamed, "Help! Police!" but nothing came out of my mouth. I stood there cowering as the window was raised, and in climbed the biggest guy I'd ever seen. He looked at me with blazing eyes, and roared:

"You've got five seconds to get out of Joe Cardone's apartment! After that you're going to start having *bad luck*!"

That's when I recognized the intruder. Semi-relief flooded over me. It wasn't a burglar. It was worse. Whenever Joe wanted to scare me, he'd tell stories about his craziest friend, a guy named Rootbeer Racinette, who was half man, half Bigfoot. I'd always figured he was exaggerating until this very moment. The person standing before me was almost seven feet tall, and his long black hair and beard looked as though he'd just stuck his finger in an electric socket. There was no doubt about it. The man, the myth, the legend, Rootbeer Racinette, had surfaced in our toilet.

"I'm Jason," I said in a small voice. "Joe's brother. Are you — uh — ?" For some reason, I had trouble making my mouth form the word — "Rootbeer?"

"Jason! Yeah!" He gave me a "friendly" slap on the back that sent me reeling into the wall. "I thought someone broke into Joe's place. It's not that hard, you know."

I watched him replace the air conditioner with

one hand. It had taken all three of us forty-five minutes to get it from the closet to the window.

"Well, I was kind of scared at first," I said with a nervous laugh. "We've had some crime in the neighborhood. Joe's car's been stolen."

Rootbeer looked shocked. *"Already?* I just parked it two minutes ago!"

I looked out to Pitt Street. There, in front of the deli, was the Camaro, gleaming like an aerodynamic black hole. *"You* had it?"

"Sure. Joe and I are really tight. We share everything. I grabbed the Camaro and took a spin down to Florida. I had some business to take care of with this guy and, wouldn't you know it, he had *bad luck."*

"But *we* had the keys!"

Rootbeer shrugged. "Oh yeah. Keys. Never use 'em."

I glanced at the window. "I can see that."

Rootbeer reached into his shirt, actually a voluminous poncho, and pulled out a crumpled paper grocery bag. "Where should I put my luggage?"

Life did this to you every so often. Here I was, so happy that the car wasn't stolen after all — I could have danced a jig, except my towel would have fallen off. How long did I get to enjoy this bliss? Less than thirty seconds before being hit with the news that this ponchoed grizzly bear was moving in.

I cleared my throat very carefully. "Uh — just how long are you planning to stay?"

Rootbeer stuck his great ugly face into his paper bag and counted up his underwear. "Four pairs. Yup. I'm here from now on."

At that moment, there was an insistent knocking at the door. "Quit talking to yourself, Jason, and let me into the can before I bust a gut!"

Rootbeer flung the door wide, and Don jumped back with a gasp. Even the unflappable Peach was staring at me as if to say, "You went into the bathroom to take a shower, and this came up out of the drain, right?"

"Ferguson, Don, this is Rootbeer Racinette. Uh — he brought the car back. Isn't that great?"

Rootbeer chased down my two roommates and awarded each one the how-do-you-do wallop. "Any pals of Joe Cardone's brother are pals of mine."

Poor Ferguson and Don alternated between terror and confusion.

"He's Joe's friend," I supplied.

"I'm here to make a change," Rootbeer announced. "My old job really took a lot out of me."

"What line of work are you thinking of getting into?" asked Don with a quiver in his voice.

"None," said Rootbeer honestly. "See, that was my whole problem. The same job, day in, day out, no excitement, no variety."

"What did you do?" ventured the Peach.

"I wrestled alligators. Don't try it. What a grind."

The three of us all agreed to take Rootbeer's advice.

Our new roommate yawned and stretched, which was a sight I won't attempt to describe. "Well, I'm going to crash for a while," he said, then threw himself down on the floor, and fell asleep instantly.

There was a second's pause, and then a mad scramble for the bathroom. The idea was that the first guy washed and dressed would be the first guy out of the apartment. Don beat us there, slammed the door, and locked it.

"No fair!" said Ferguson. "You said you wanted to sleep in this morning."

"I've got to go to work!" came Don's voice through the door.

"You don't have a job," I retorted. I didn't, either, but who was thinking straight?

"Yeah, but I have to find one. I want to start pounding the pavement at nine sharp."

"He's just scared," I told Ferguson.

"I don't blame him."

Rootbeer slumbered on, his poncho draped around him like a blanket. It was a patchwork affair, made of what looked like old flannel pajamas, and it was big enough for two of him. I laughed nervously. What a concept! Two of Rootbeer would get its own area code from the phone company. *Three* of Rootbeer — well, I didn't know too much about physics, but three might have so much gravitational attraction that his atoms would collapse in on each other, and he would achieve critical mass — a tiny neutron star in a poncho.

The summer was heating up, but even as the mercury crawled past 95° F, Don and I stayed away from the nice cool apartment. We bought a *Toronto Star*, and found a reasonably shaded park bench on which to begin our job search.

We never got to the want ads. En route to the classifieds, a headline caught my eye:

66

"Rootbeer!" I blurted out.

Don jumped. *"Where?"*

"This article! It's him!"

The piece stated that the disgruntled employee suspected of being the culprit was an alligator wrestler fired for being too hard on the alligators.

"I don't like this, Jason," quavered Don. "Maybe Joe could kick him out. Call Europe."

I had to laugh. "What am I supposed to say? 'Hello, Europe? Could you please put Joe Cardone on?' And even if I could reach Joe, then what? *He's* the idiot who invited Rootbeer in the first place. He probably said 'Come anytime,' and forgot to mention he'd be gone all summer. Knowing Joe, he gave the guy *carte blanche* — the place, the car, *us* — let's hope Rootbeer doesn't believe in human sacrifice."

Don slapped the paper. "Look what he does when he's disgruntled! Can you imagine when he gets really mad? It's bound to happen! Nobody stays gruntled forever!"

"Look," I said, "pretty soon we'll both be working, so we'll only be hanging around the place at night. Rootbeer'll be doing his own thing, and we'll hardly ever see him. For all we know, he might pick up and blow off to Florida or somewhere again. Joe always talked about Rootbeer being flaky. So don't worry about it."

I sounded confident, but that still didn't give me the guts to go into the apartment. For lunch, we split a small order of McDonald's french fries, all we could afford on $5.83 per person per week. Between the hunger and the heat, we were limp as rags by the time Ferguson stepped off the Bathurst bus and found us sitting on the front stoop.

"Just enjoying the sunshine," Don told him.

"Oh sure," said the Peach. "And it's got nothing to do with the fact that you don't want any one-on-one with our guest, Mr. Racinette."

There's safety in numbers, and we had as many as we were going to get. I'd have felt a little more secure being backed up by a crack platoon of Marines, but there are times you just have to go for it. Besides, if we didn't eat something, Don and I were going to faint. "Let's get up there! I'm starved!"

We paused to watch Plotnick burst out and net a hubcap from a speeding station wagon.

I waved. "Nice catch."

Waddling back to the deli, our landlord scowled at me. "Mr. Cardone, I don't want to mix in, but I think you should know there's a gorilla in your apartment. Remember, no pets."

"Come on, Mr. Plotnick," I said, "you know it's a person."

"That's your opinion," said Plotnick. "Another houseguest?"

I nodded.

"What a host you are, Mr. Cardone. Just so you know, when I open my hotel, I'm going to start charging by the head."

We ran upstairs, but paused before opening the door. I was in agony. What if that lunatic had trashed the apartment? I clicked the lock, and we went inside. The place looked exactly as it had when we'd left this morning, only Rootbeer had picked himself up off the floor, and was seated on the couch, watching television.

He looked up at us. "Hi. I hope you don't mind. I ate your food."

"No problem," I said. "There's plenty for everybody." Ravenously I went to the kitchen to investigate the prospects for dinner. That's when I found out that when Rootbeer Racinette eats your food, he *really* eats your food. All of it, right down to the last cracker. Even Mrs. Peach's bran hockey pucks were gone. We were bare to the walls.

"Uh — Rootbeer," I said cautiously, "what happened to all the food?"

"I ate it. That's okay, isn't it?"

"But we had eight cans of soup," I protested.

Rootbeer rubbed an area at the vague epicenter of the poncho. "I love soup."

I began opening cupboards at random. Even the salt and pepper shakers were empty. Don and Ferguson were in the kitchen, too, now, searching.

"What about the cereal?" lamented Don, who had gotten the smaller half of our lunch fries. "We had Snappy-Wappies! We had Toasty-Flakes!"

"Breakfast is the most important meal of the day," said Rootbeer. He stood up, his face all concern. "Hey, this isn't a problem, is it?"

"Well," I said, choosing my words carefully. I didn't want to insult Rootbeer and end up with that alligator guy's BMW — at the bottom of the Everglades. "You kind of caught us on a bad week. The fact is, we're all flat broke. We were depending on this food to last till payday."

"Okay," said Rootbeer cheerfully, "I'm broke, too. I guess I'll have to work."

Ferguson risked a complaint. "Your getting a job won't help us now. We have no dinner."

"Yeah, I feel bad about that," said Rootbeer. "You guys are going to have to hang out for a couple of hours."

A terrible hush fell over the three of us. What kind of job, lasting a couple of hours and yielding instant cash, could Rootbeer be talking about? It didn't make us any more confident when he said he had to wait until it got dark. But how could we face him and say, "Rootbeer, which bank are you going to knock off?" because on the chance, however slight, that his plans were lawful and honest, he'd be pretty insulted. And even though we'd only just met him this morning, we'd already learned that people who insulted Rootbeer Racinette invariably ran into Bad Luck.

"I'll need one of you to come with me," Rootbeer announced when the sun began to set.

That did it. Don suddenly developed a terrible headache, and Ferguson locked himself in the bathroom, obviously with no intention of coming out. I could have made a fuss, demanded we draw straws or flip a coin, but I didn't. It was Joe's apartment and Joe's friend, and the job of going with him fell to me.

Just before nine, Rootbeer declared the time was right. I followed him, my empty stomach rumbling ominously, as though it knew that my next meal was going to be served at Chez Penitentiary, on a tin plate.

We got into the car, and Rootbeer drove at a

hundred miles an hour to an area of town even seedier than Pitt Street, if such a thing was possible. We parked in front of an old building that was in the process of either being torn down or collapsing, and Rootbeer started rummaging through the pile of debris, coming up with a long rotted two-by-four. This he carried over his shoulder, like a soldier with an eight-foot rifle, to a dumpy establishment on the corner with a neon sign that just read *Bar*.

"Wait here," he told me, and disappeared inside.

About five seconds later, a booming voice bellowed, *"Twenty bucks says you can't hurt me with a shot in the stomach with this two-by-four!"*

I almost died. There was a roar of enthusiasm from the bar, and out onto the street poured eighteen people, Rootbeer in the lead. He collected twenty dollars each from the participants, who were in a spirited argument over who would get to swing the heavy piece of lumber.

He handed the money to me. "Hold this."

"For God's sake, Rootbeer," I quavered, "you can't go through with this! You'll get killed! Not to mention if we lose, we can't pay off five cents of that money!"

"Not so loud!" whispered Rootbeer. "People don't like to bet when they know there's no money to pay them. They get mad."

By this time, the eighteen were taking practice swings with the two-by-four. The whistle of the board through the air was making me queasy, and I watched in a daze as the group elected some guy who had once tried out for the Yankees to take the home run swing.

There are times in your life when you see something so totally amazing you forget how scared you are and try to make the moment last, because you know you'll never see anything quite like it again. Whenever I think back to that night, I always see it in super slo-mo, although it was really over in a flash. Rootbeer stood there like a mighty redwood, feet planted, stomach tense under his poncho. The almost-Yankee swung for the upper deck. The board slammed into Rootbeer's abdomen with a thump that echoed through the streets. The wood splintered. I felt the sidewalk lurch, but Rootbeer didn't move. He didn't even flinch.

He started to whistle, and glanced around the circle of shocked faces. "Nice meeting everybody. We'd better get going. 'Bye."

The three of us, me, Rootbeer, and the money, climbed back into the Camaro. Rootbeer indicated that I should drive, and I was overjoyed to take off out of there. Neither of us spoke, so I figured I had to break the ice.

"Rootbeer, that was amazing — "

"*Aaaahhh!!!*" he shrieked in a bone-chilling voice that nearly put me up a telephone pole.

"Are you okay?"

"*Aaaahhh!!!*"

Now I knew why he'd needed one of us to go with him. Somebody had to do the driving while he screamed.

"*Aaaahhh!!!*"

He indicated by sign language that I should pull in at a grocery store, and sent me in to shop while he remained in the car, howling. Even in the frozen food section, over the Muzak, I could hear the echoes from the parking lot. About ten minutes later, Rootbeer joined me, cheerful as ever, as though he hadn't been in the throes of agony thirty seconds ago. We bought $150 worth of groceries — enough to last even Rootbeer until Friday.

"What happened?" asked Don when we got back.

A five-hour explanation formed in my head. "Nothing," I said. They wouldn't have believed me, anyway.

The next morning we awoke to find Rootbeer Racinette lying dead on the floor.

We didn't even know at first, because he always flopped down to sleep wherever he happened to be standing. So we tiptoed around, careful not to wake him up as we showered and dressed.

"At least he isn't snoring," whispered Don. "Did you hear him last night? I thought the building was going to come down. The Phantom was knocking on the wall."

The Peach bent over Rootbeer. "The reason he isn't snoring," he said, his face pale, "is because he isn't breathing."

We freaked out. The three of us crawled all over Rootbeer, poking, and prodding, and feeling for a heartbeat that wasn't there. He was dead as a mackerel.

I admit it. I burst into tears, blubbering out the whole story of last night. "It's all my fault!" I wailed. "If I'd stopped him, he'd be alive now! Joe would have stopped him! But I let him do it! And now he's dead, because of internal injuries or something! What are we going to do?"

Ferguson shook his head. "Call the police, of course."

"No police!" came a howl through the ventilation duct. This was followed by pounding footsteps on the stairs, and then Plotnick burst onto the scene, red-faced and wild-eyed.

He took in the situation with a horrified gasp. "Oi! How could this happen to me?"

"To *you*?!" I shrieked. "To *you*?! A guy is *dead*!"

"Okay, okay," said Plotnick. "We're in this together. We need to be reasonable. Let me think." His brow furrowed, and unfurrowed. "All right. Take him out, throw him in a field, and to hell with him, God rest his soul!"

I was horrified. "We can't do that!"

"Yes we can. I don't want hassles over this. First police, then the coroner, then the reporters — no. Not in my building."

"Look, Mr. Plotnick," I argued, "if we throw the body in a field, the police will suspect foul play. When they trace it, they won't just hassle us. They'll toss us in jail!"

"I'm an old man," Plotnick shrugged. "Maybe by the time they trace it, I'll be dead."

But by then, the Peach had already dialed 911, and the police were on their way.

The next hour was a nightmare. I must have told the story about the two-by-four twenty times, first to the police, then to the reporters, then to our fellow tenants. Plotnick went to lie down, and the officers, seeing an elderly man obviously overcome by emotion, were brief and kind. They assumed that he was upset over the untimely death, never guessing that his collapse was due to their own presence.

I was destroyed as I watched the uniformed attendants carry Rootbeer's body on two stretchers out to the ambulance. Don, Ferguson, and I followed like an honor guard. God's Grandmother sobbed uncontrollably, and Wayne Gretzky's Sister dabbed at her eyes with a napkin. The Assassin removed his hat respectfully. Even Plotnick joined us, coming out of hiding, since the law was gone. The back doors of the ambulance swallowed Rootbeer up, and the vehicle pulled away slowly. There was no siren, no rush. This was Rootbeer's last ride.

The ambulance got as far as the corner. Then the white reverse lights came on, and it backed up, coming to a stop in front of the deli. The doors swung wide, and out stepped Rootbeer Racinette, fresh as a daisy.

"He's alive!" cried Don.

The three of us made a run at Rootbeer, catching him in a joyful embrace, blubbering incoherently. Plotnick launched into a tantrum because the police had come to his building for nothing. Our neighbors cheered, and the two attendants craned their necks out the ambulance windows to stare at the man they had pronounced dead just a few minutes earlier.

Rootbear stretched expansively. "What's everybody so excited about?"

I couldn't believe it. "You were *dead*, Rootbeer! No heartbeat or anything! And I figured because of that hit you took last night . . ." My voice trailed off.

The ex-corpse looked mystified for a second,

then laughed airily. "I'm into Manchurian Bush Meditation. I learned it from a guru in Buffalo. Your heart slows down to five or six beats a minute, which is probably what fooled you guys. It was an honest mistake."

"I'll give you an honest mistake, you degenerate!" raged Plotnick. "If they put you in the ground before you wake up — *that's* an honest mistake!"

Rootbeer shrugged. "No hard feelings."

The ambulance attendants had hard feelings. They left a lot of rubber on Pitt Street before squealing away onto Bathurst. Plotnick had hard feelings. He stormed back into the deli and sulked behind the counter, sharpening his meat fork. The three of us had hard feelings, too, but to the bizarre giant in the poncho, we didn't dare say anything.

Six

The envelope was postmarked Biarritz, and contained a photograph of my brother frolicking on the beach with a fabulous brunette. *Me and Yvette on the French Riviera. P.S. I forgot to tell you that Rootbeer might be dropping by. He sometimes does this thing where it looks like he's dead, but it's really okay.*

Rootbeer was already gone by the time we woke up that morning. None of us had heard him leave, which seemed kind of strange. Not noticing Rootbeer was like not noticing Europe. There was no note, but wherever he was, at least he'd left the car this time. It was parked in front of the deli.

"Maybe he's gone for good," said the Peach.

"Shhh!" admonished Don. "We don't want to jinx ourselves."

I threw down the Employment section in disgust. "Well, Don, it looks like we blew our chance at having important jobs when we got canned making bubble wands."

We'd just bundled the Peach off to dumb Plastics Unlimited with a sarcastic "Have a nice day at work, Honey." The two of us had gotten up early to prepare him a brown bag lunch consisting of the tidbits we could find in the trash dumpster outside, but he mentioned something about lunch meetings, and left us our garbage, which was starting to smell as we pored over the paper.

"If he's going to keep making us look like idiots, the least he can do is fall for our jokes," was Don's opinion.

"All the good summer jobs are taken," I complained. "We're too late for anything decent. I wish your uncle had warned us he only needed feeders for five days."

"How was he supposed to know the great Doctor of Fuzzology was going to stick his nose into everything? Hey, can I type eighty words a minute?"

I had to laugh. "You'd be lucky to do eighty words a month." Don typed with his right index finger: click . . . click . . . click . . .

Don was undaunted. "Wow! This is a fantastic job! Your own office, a secretary, great money, short hours — we should call these guys."

I looked over his shoulder to his pointing finger. "That's for 'Brain Surgeon.' "

"Oh. Nah, too gucky." But he stuck to the job search, and by ten-thirty, he was gainfully employed. True, he was a delivery boy for the local supermarket, but it was more than I'd been able to come up with. Still, when he rode up in front of 1 Pitt Street on the supermarket bicycle, I just couldn't stop laughing. For starters, it was one of those old-style bikes, and it was huge — Don was on tiptoe when each pedal reached its lowest point. There was a giant pink basket in front of the handlebars, and another one behind the seat. And a bell, great big, shiny, and silver. Here was Mr. Big City Cool, riding around on a bike he wouldn't be caught dead on in Owen Sound.

"What's the bell for?" I called from the stoop. "Just in case you get stuck behind a Maserati and you have to alert the driver to let you pass?"

"Go ahead and laugh!" snarled Don. "I absolutely refuse to have Peachfuzz paying my bills!"

It was the first *really* sweltering day of the summer, and the air was heavy and humid. I felt sorry for Don, who would probably be half dead by dinnertime in all that heat. As soon as he had pedaled out of sight, I escaped back up to the air conditioning. Just inside the door, I paused, looking distastefully at the Employment section, lying open on the beanbag chair. Even thinking about the tiny black print made my eyes bug out. My hands were filthy with ink from the newsprint.

Looking for a job was harder than working. I scanned the first couple of ads. *Experience required, Experience required.* How are you supposed to get experience if no one'll hire you because you don't have experience?

When you really hate what you're doing, you notice stuff you normally wouldn't pick up on. For the first time, I realized what total slobs Ferguson and Don were. Our sleeping arrangements consisted of the bed, the couch, and the beanbag chair, with Rootbeer taking the floor directly over where he happened to be standing the instant he declared himself officially tired. The Peach had left the bed unmade, and Mr. Wonderful's couch looked like a bomb site — sheets and pillows all over the place, wadded-up sweat socks and underwear. This was the guy who thought a few wrinkles in a shirt was a disaster. Apparently his nattiness only extended to those articles of clothing that went on the *outside*, visible to the casual observer.

A few minutes of tidying up wouldn't kill the job search. And who wanted to live in a pigsty?

Pigsty. That was my mother's word. It referred, usually, to my room. I pulled up short in some alarm. In the great summer of independence, here I was doing *voluntarily* what I could usually get out of at home. Oh, no!

Well, at least at home, when the debris piled up above my nostrils, I could always hang out in another room. Here one room was *it*. It was only common sense to keep it neat.

The problem with straightening up was that I noticed other things about the apartment. Not only was it messy, but it was also pretty dirty and dusty. Joe's vacuum cleaner was our old one from Owen Sound, and it was incredibly loud — I was eight years old before I finally figured out it wasn't a monster come to eat the family. Plotnick was banging on the pipes and screaming for me to turn it off, but I forged on until I'd covered every square inch except the hallowed ground on which sat

Rootbeer's paper bag of underwear. I didn't want to fool with *that* no matter how bad the dust got.

I noticed that I'd already used up a complete hour of job-hunting time.

Then came the mopping stage. I doubted Joe had ever mopped in his life, but, just in case, I checked in the broom closet for cleaner. I opened the door and gawked.

There, in the dim red glow of a safe-light, squatted Rootbeer Racinette, developing photographic prints in various trays of chemicals. I slammed the door so fast that, a second later, it seemed that the whole thing had been merely a hallucination. When the beating of my heart slowed down a little, I steeled myself and knocked politely. "Uh — Rootbeer?"

"Yeah?" came the voice from within.

"What're you doing?"

"Making some prints."

"You're a photographer?"

"A guy needs distraction from all the pressures, you know," came the voice. "People are dropping like flies from executive burnout."

I stared at the closet door. "You're not an executive."

"That makes it even riskier," Rootbeer replied. "If you've got a job, you know what to do every day. But me — no sooner do I get up than the decisions start. I could feel the stress eating away at me."

"But all that stuff in there must have cost hundreds!" I protested.

"Worrying about money is the number-one cause of burnout " said Rootbeer. "So I spent it all.

And I feel great! Hey, you can look at my first picture."

Watching Rootbeer crawl out of a cramped closet is like when someone opens a suitcase and out comes a full-grown bull elephant. In his hand, he clutched a gleaming wet 8" × 10" glossy and proudly held it out before me.

"It's white!" I blurted out.

Rootbeer examined the blank photograph. "Hmmm. I guess you exposed it when you opened the door."

Oh, no! I'd ruined Rootbeer Racinette's picture. It was as though I'd walked up and infected him with executive burnout. "Sorry," I quavered.

"Oh, don't worry," said Rootbeer. "I gotta have a hobby, but nobody says I gotta be any good at it." He held his picture between his thumb and forefinger and began to blow on it softly.

His whole roll came out exactly like that, but this first picture was his favorite, so up it went on the wall, right over the stereo. Rootbeer signed it with a green crayon that appeared out of the poncho.

"It looks great," I said.

"And see how relaxed and happy I am," added Rootbeer, and he fell into Manchurian Bush Meditation on the spot.

I mopped as best I could, working around Rootbeer, and by the time I'd taken out the garbage and mailed a couple of letters, it was four-ten, time to go back to the job search. I paused. Four-ten was almost four-fifteen, which was just a quarter hour before four-thirty. Most people are winding down their day by then — some even knock off

82

half an hour early, especially those important enough to be responsible for hiring new guys. In other words, not only would I be wasting my time in applying for anything now, but I'd actually be *hurting my chances* by pestering people so late.

I should have been disappointed; I felt great. And after all, it wasn't as though I'd *wasted* the day. The apartment was spotless (another of my mother's words — watch it, Cardone).

Speak of the devil — the phone rang. My mother.

"What are you doing home? I knew it! You're sick!"

I managed a high-pitched giggle. "I'm not sick. It's my day off." Every day was my day off.

"Well, I was just going to leave a message on your machine to let you know that your father and I will be at the Murphys' tonight in case you need us."

The meaning was clear. If I happened to decide that I wanted to go home during the two hours that they'd be out, I could call them at the Murphys' for instant rescue.

"I won't need you," I assured her. I glanced at the dead rhinoceros lying on our floor. "Everything's fine. 'Bye."

It was unnerving to be with Rootbeer when he was meditating. Sure, I knew he wasn't dead, but it was scary to be in the same room with somebody lying there not breathing. So I went for a walk. You can't spend all day cooped up anyway. It isn't healthy.

I walked up Bathurst in the direction of where Don said Jessica's place was. If I could accidentally-on-purpose run into her, I could strike up a conversation, and maybe work in there how Don had tried to take off after the Moontrix head bonk scene. I would portray myself as the strong, silent type — not *too* nice, but with a manly sense of responsibility. Of course, Don was my friend, and you weren't supposed to screw up your friends. But he didn't deserve Jessica anyway. He hadn't even called her yet. And besides, if I somehow managed to steal her away from Mr. Wonderful, he'd have another girlfriend in nothing flat. On the other hand, waiting for someone to go for Cardone could take *years*!

I looked from window to window, up and down the street, half believing it wasn't a waste of time. Did I expect a golden aura to be emanating from the building that housed Jessica and her legs?

Finally I returned to the stoop in front of 1 Pitt Street to wait for Ferguson and Don to get home from work. I was already sweating like crazy. The air was like vaporized oatmeal. I waved at God's Grandmother as she jogged by, energetic, cool, and sweat-free.

I saw the pink baskets first, piled high with bags of groceries, plodding their way through the heavy traffic. Between them pedaled a very hot and tired-looking Don Champion. Suddenly a long, silver, stretch limousine shot out of nowhere and passed Don too close. Mr. Wonderful swerved to avoid it, and put himself out of control. His front wheel touched the curb, and the bicycle dropped out of view. But I could see groceries flying in all directions. Bottles, cans, fruits, and vegetables bounced off the roofs and hoods of other cars. Oblivious to this havoc, the driver of the limo turned onto Pitt Street and pulled up right in front of me. The door opened, and out climbed the Peach.

"Thanks for the ride, Mr. Robb. See you tomorrow."

Don was on his feet by now, examining a carton of eggs. He saw who it was getting out of the limo just as twelve yolks spilled out of the package onto his shirt.

"PEACHFUZZ!!!"

Repugnant as the thought of handing money over to Plotnick was, we decided to eat in the deli. There was just so much tuna fish and peanut butter a guy could stomach, and we had enough cash for two corned beef sandwiches between the three of us. The Peach and I waited out front for Don, who had to roll the mangled delivery bicycle back to the supermarket.

"Well, write off one bike and one job," he told us when he got home. "Guess who just got fired, thanks to the fuzzy skin of a certain fruit I could name? Not to mention that it could have been me bent into a pretzel along with the bike!"

Ferguson shrugged. "It's *your* uncle's car. And besides, if that bicycle had been designed with the center of balance a little farther forward — "

"Didn't you explain that it wasn't your fault?" I asked Don quickly.

"They didn't believe me. They wouldn't even pay me for today because of the bike. That's the only part that bothers me. I was going to quit that bogus slavery anyway."

"Why?"

Don snorted. "Are you kidding? The pay stinks, and you have to ride around on that idiot bicycle, sweating your guts out while little kids follow you singing, 'Hey, Mr. Grocery Man!' And you're a target for every dog and psychopath in the neighborhood. This one kid — five years old, tops! — yells, 'Hey, Mr. Grocery Man, think fast,' and hurls this huge dirt bomb at my face. But that's not the real crusher. Check this out." He paused for effect. "For lunch I grabbed some Doritos and hung out in the park. So I catch a rap with these two great-looking girls. Everything's going terrific, and they're complaining about how they've got nothing to do this summer, and I'm thinking *we're in*. Just as I'm about to suggest we all get together, they see the bike, and it's game over. They couldn't stop *laughing* long enough for me to ask them out. I mean, I refuse to hold any job that messes with my love life!"

"I guess that rules out the priesthood," Ferguson commented seriously.

"Wait a second!" That was me. "What about Jessica?"

Don shrugged carelessly. "Do you seriously expect me to spend this whole summer with *one* girl? We're here for freedom, remember?"

Those of us who were not Mr. Wonderful felt a flash of extremely unfriendly annoyance. "Aren't we getting a little greedy here?" I hoped I sounded socially aware rather than just plain jealous. "I mean, you haven't even called Jessica, and you're already planning a harem."

"I have to play it cool," said Don reasonably.

"It's good for them to sit by the phone. Keeps 'em humble."

"Let's eat," said Ferguson.

"Hey, listen," I said as we seated ourselves at the usual booth. "When we get upstairs, there's going to be a blank piece of paper up on the wall. Act like you love it."

They looked up at me questioningly, but by that time Plotnick was already bearing down on us, shaking his head. "Mr. Champion, I'm very disappointed in you. Picking up girls on the job? No wonder you got fired."

"That had nothing to do with it," said Don sulkily.

I stared at the landlord. "How could you know all that?"

"Well," said Plotnick evasively, "you were talking outside — "

"Do you read lips?"

He shrugged. "A little hobby. And you, Mr. Peach, I must say I'm impressed with your choice of travel arrangements. Riding around like a tycoon in a great big car. You're doing very well for yourself for someone who is just only a houseguest."

"Thank you," said the Peach.

"Hey, Mr. Plotnick," I piped up. "The spaghetti special looks great. What do you think?"

He snorted haughtily. "The food at the Olympiad Delicatessen is among the finest in the world."

"The problem is," I continued, "we've only got five bucks. But we promise to give you the rest on Friday."

Plotnick grabbed the menu from my hand and

made an elaborate show of reading the cover. "What a relief! For a minute I thought it said Salvation Army. Nobody has a charge account here, least of all a couple of unemployed nogoodniks."

"Hey!" protested Don. "I went by the car wash on my way home, and they said they'd probably have a job for me starting tomorrow. So there!"

Plotnick clasped his hands in ecstasy. "A car wash attendant living in my building! The *prestige*!"

"Listen! I'll be a specialist! The chrome polisher!"

Plotnick fanned himself with his apron. "It's too much for an old man! Hey, Mr. Champion — big deal."

"Come on, Mr. Plotnick," coaxed Ferguson. "I definitely have a job, and I can pay you on Friday."

Our landlord held firm. "For all we know, the world could end on Thursday."

"What good would money do you then?" the Peach persisted.

"I would die happier."

Ordering two corned beef on rye, cut in thirds.

I went to the car wash with Don the next morning, but they only needed one chrome polisher. Too many sub-compacts, not enough chrome. So Don started work, and I picked up the paper and went home.

I had just buried myself in the Employment section when Rootbeer burst out of the broom closet, waving pictures.

"Hey, Jason, check it out."

Thirty-six high-contrast extreme close-ups of a cockroach.

"Where — where did you take these?"

"Right in the closet," crowed Rootbeer, blowing on the prints. "Talk about convenient!"

I emptied half a can of bug spray into the apartment. Even with the window wide open, it hung in the air like fog. Then I remembered what my mother went through the year the ants got in. She had to empty the kitchen cupboards, spray around, wash every dish, plate, cup, saucer, glass, knife, fork, and spoon, check all the food, move the fridge, ditto the stove, poison the drains, and then put everything back. I followed it all, step by painstaking step.

It interrupted my job search for a day and a half. Grunting and groaning, I pushed the refrigerator back into its place and plugged it in.

Rootbeer looked up from the electronic flash he was attaching to his camera. "Seems like a lot to go through for one little cockroach," he commented — he, who could have lifted the fridge with his little finger and saved me a quadruple hernia.

"There's no such thing as one cockroach," I croaked, in a very tired imitation of my mother's pep talk from the ant infestation. "If there's one, there are a hundred. And if you give them time to start having babies, forget it."

"But there *was* only one. I brought him in myself. Found him in the garbage outside. He looked photogenic."

Then, to add insult to injury, the photogenic cockroach had the gall to stroll right across the carpet in front of me. After all that bug spray, all those traps, and all that poison, he was perky as anything. Who did he think he was — Rasputin? I hit him with the newspaper, and he perked no more. And by the time I cooled off, it was after two o'clock. A lot of people take off Friday afternoons in the summer. And besides, there were bug guts all over the Employment section. Yech.

It was payday, and money animated apartment 2C like wind in the sails of a three-masted schooner. It was only Ferguson's salary plus two days chrome polishing pay from Don, but it meant the end of $5.86 per person per week, and it seemed like a fortune.

Don was bouncing around the place, hooting and laughing, because Ferguson had a date.

"I believe in miracles!" he shouted, spraying his cologne at the Peach, who was trying to get ready. "There *is* a woman ugly enough and desperate enough to waste a Friday night on Peachfuzz!"

Ferguson just smiled and combed his hair.

"What are *we* doing tonight?" I asked Don.

Mr. Wonderful reached for the phone. "I think Jessica's cooled her heels long enough. And maybe she can scare up a friend for you." He dialed. "Hello, Jess? It's Don Champion. How've you been? . . ."

Ferguson headed out the door.

"Hey, you want the car?" I offered.

"No, thanks. We can take the bus. See you later." He leaned back in towards Don and called, "Tell her I'll be there in five minutes." And then he was gone.

Don didn't catch it at all, and it took a few seconds to sink in with me.

"You've got plans, eh?" Don was saying. "Well, break 'em. . . . Oh, you can't. Well, that's no problem. . . . Nah, don't worry about it. Later." He hung up. "Bummer. She's already got a date."

It was starting to hit me. "I — I think I know who — he said — and she said — uh — " I grabbed Don and we raced into the bathroom to the window. There was the Peach, wending his way up Bathurst.

"Impossible," said Don firmly. "No chance."

But two minutes later, Ferguson reappeared, hand in hand with Jessica Lincoln.

Don was very calm. "There's only one explanation. Jessica is insane. Poor girl. Good thing I didn't get mixed up with her."

"You didn't call her all week," I said in a feeble attempt to defend the Peach. What the hell was going on here? Now she was dating *Ferguson*? How did that happen? Did I miss something? I sat down heavily on the edge of the bathtub, my hopes for Jessica completely dashed. I couldn't imagine what she was thinking about, but I knew exactly what she *wasn't* thinking about. Me. I must have really caught her eye that night. Maybe my shirt had the same pattern as the wallpaper at Moontrix.

"Well," shrugged Don, heading back into the living room, "I always knew Peachfuzz was an idiot, but I didn't think he was a sleazebag. As for Jessica — her loss. Now — what are we going to do tonight?"

"Why don't you stay home and help me with my stamp collection?" asked Rootbeer from the beanbag chair.

"What stamp collection?" I asked, wandering to

the sofa and slumping down on it, face first.

"It's my new hobby. Stamp collecting is a great way to relax and get my mind off all the pressures."

"But your hobby is photography," I protested. "What about the darkroom in the broom closet?"

He dismissed this with a wave of his beefy hand. "Can't see a thing in there. It's dark." He shook his shaggy head. "I don't think this is going to be very relaxing. Everything is so *small*!" He held up a tweezers, which looked like a straight pin in his mammoth paw. "I'm supposed to pick up stamps with this; I can't even pick up *this*! I asked the guy to sell me bigger stamps, but he didn't have any."

I was stunned. "But — but you were still snapping pictures two hours ago!"

Rootbeer shrugged. "The guy at the pawnshop gave me big bucks for the enlarger."

"Oh," I said. Come to think of it, I'd gone out for some air that afternoon, mostly to parade myself up and down Bathurst where stupid Jessica lived. It was half an hour, tops. But somewhere in there, Rootbeer must have left the apartment a photographer, and returned a stamp collector. It boggled the mind but, then again, so did Rootbeer.

On the way out, Don posed the question. "What is he relaxing *from*?"

"Executive burnout."

We giggled all the way downstairs.

"I scouted out the perfect place for us to eat," said Don as we hit the street. "It's right here on Pitt Street, on the other side of Bathurst. It's called the Pop Bistro, and the sign says, 'Blues Nitely,' N-I-T-E-L-Y. Is that city cool, or what?"

The Pop Bistro was in a building that looked like

a nice version of 1 Pitt Street. The paint was fresh, the brick had been sandblasted, and new aluminum windows gleamed.

I turned to Don. "We'd better be careful. I'll bet this place looked exactly like Plotnick's until somebody started breaking stairs."

As we made for the Pop Bistro's front door, we stopped to admire the pink neon Eiffel Tower on the club's sign.

Don sighed deeply. "This is going to be great. We should have bought berets."

As he reached for the door handle, a distant voice called, "No-o-o-o!" We wheeled to see Plotnick rushing across the street after us, waving his meat fork. By the time he reached us, he was gray and gasping. "Mr. Cardone! Mr. Champion! You can't go in there!"

We stared. "Why?"

"It's no good! You'll get gas! And heartburn! And food poisoning!"

I swallowed hard. "Mr. Plotnick, no offense, but we're going to eat wherever we please. Two days ago, someone wouldn't sell us three lousy plates of spaghetti on credit, and he's not getting another chance. We need to relax tonight, so please leave us alone."

The meat fork made a dangerous arc in front of my face. "You can't relax in there! It's crazy, with people packed like sardines — you'll come out, you'll have high blood pressure!"

Don brightened. "That's what we want. We're looking for some action."

"It's boring!" Plotnick raged. "You'll hate it! Come have dinner in my restaurant."

"No way," I said.

Don looked at our agitated landlord. "Mr. Plotnick, what do you have against this place?"

"It's owned by a money-grubber!" Both of us stared directly at him. "Not me! Hamish! A no-good, a lowlife! For thirty years I've known Hamish, and never once has he done a nice thing for another person! His building and restaurant used to be just like mine, and *now* look what he's done with it!"

Don shrugged. "It's nice."

"Nice! Nice! That bandit! He gouges big rents from his tenants, big prices from his customers, and he's making a fortune — I could take poison!"

"I get it," I said. "You're jealous."

Plotnick glared. "I deny this! It's a filthy lie!"

I set my jaw. "We're eating here, Mr. Plotnick. And whatever this guy Hamish charges, bandit or not, it's got to be cheaper than dealing with you."

With his free hand, Plotnick tore open the Bistro door, screamed, "They're under-age!" and, with a triumphant look, started back to the deli.

I stared at the sign that read, *No One Under 19 Will Be Admitted.*

Don gazed with a forlorn expression at Plotnick's receding back. "We weren't going in there to drink," he said sadly. "We just wanted some food and some 'Blues Nitely.' "

We went back to 1 Pitt Street, picked up the car, and started to cruise the Harborfront area. We found a restaurant that was fairly cool but not too expensive-looking, because our cash was still limited.

No sooner were we seated than Don's radar was up, scanning the vicinity for a likely female. It took about three seconds.

"Bingo," he said smugly. "She makes Jessica look like a train wreck."

I wouldn't go that far, but she was pretty nice. The problem was she was sitting with her parents.

Don cast her his best Meet Mr. Wonderful look, and she responded with a dazzling, green-eyed, red-haired smile that practically knocked the two of us over in our chairs. I frowned at Don resentfully. It must be nice to attract female attention with one well-placed glance. The girl's father noticed the romantic communication, and scowled Don down. I beamed my approval. It went on like that all through dinner, she and Don trading vibes, and the parents trying to freeze Don out. I kept score, secretly rooting for Mom and Dad.

I was choking down food like crazy, because Don insisted that we had to pull even with them by the dessert stage, and I was half a chicken behind.

"You could snort all this up your nose, and it wouldn't do you any good," I said, mouth full. "Those parents aren't going to let you anywhere near her."

"Keep eating and leave that to me," Don mumbled, while sucking in an entire bowlful of linguini. "Check the table in front of her. She's had three Cokes. When she heads for the can, she's mine."

These Mr. Wonderful strategies — they sound so stupid, but they work! It unfolded just like he said. She disappeared down the hallway to the restrooms, and Don was behind her like a Secret Service bodyguard. Her dad wheeled in his chair and shot me a look that would melt lead.

I shrugged apologetically.

"Kiki!" chortled Don gleefully. "The Peach-fuzzes of this world can only get so far before the real Champions rise to the surface! A Kiki beats a Jessica any day!"

By the dim light of the dashboard, Don pored over a cocktail napkin. On it was written *Kiki: 555-2461* in red lipstick. Beside the signature was the glossy red impression of lips kissing the paper.

"Anybody named Kiki has to be awesome, but her — wow! And if I say so myself, it was true artistry getting this number, right under her parents' noses! Not bad at all."

"You'd better be careful," I advised Don. "That father looks like he patrols under her bedroom window with a blunderbuss."

"He'll come around," said Don serenely.

"Yeah!" I snapped. "He'll come around the corner to see what he shot!"

"Listen, it's not just the number; it's the momentum! These things come in waves, Jason! This is just what we needed." He slapped the note for emphasis. "*This* is the break that's going to turn our summer around. Mark my words, from this moment on, everything is going to be perfect!"

Suddenly I was blinded by red lights in the rear-view mirror. I craned my neck to see a police car tailing us. I pulled over, and one officer got out and examined the Camaro. When he knelt to check the license plate, it hit me in one instant of exquisite horror — we'd forgotten to call the police to report the "stolen" car had never really been stolen at all.

We were under arrest.

My gibbered-out explanation of why we were in the stolen vehicle not only made us look like criminals, but stupid criminals to boot. Even Don didn't believe me, and he knew I was telling the truth. Let's face it — "Car — Rootbeer — Florida — Joe — alligators — I didn't do anything!" wasn't about to convince the police to let us go.

We sat at the desk while the arresting officer spoke on the phone across the room.

Don craned his neck around the station house. "Don't worry, Jason. We're definitely the best-dressed guys who got arrested tonight. Good thing we wore our new clothes."

I couldn't believe it. "Are you nuts? We're in jail! What difference does it make what we're wearing?"

"Don't be dumb. We're a couple of clean-cut guys. If we looked sleazy, they'd probably lock us up while they checked out our story."

Our cop hung up the phone and came over, looking grim. "I'm going to lock you up while I check out your story. Empty your pockets."

Stunned, we handed over everything we could find in the new clothes that made us so respectable, and would keep us out of the clink.

They took our wallets and watches and Don's gold chain. They even took the note on the cocktail napkin. Don pleaded with them, but the officer said rules were rules.

"You take good care of that!" cried Don.

Then we were escorted through the dingy, chaotic halls of the police station to a windowless interrogation room, and left there.

I turned to Don. " 'From this moment on, everything's going to be perfect!' " I mimicked savagely.

"If they lose Kiki's telephone number," Don promised, "I'm going to *sue* the Toronto Police Department!"

"For what?" I snarled.

"Wrongful misplacement of an important document!" Mr. Wonderful declared.

"Napkin-napping would be more like it."

"I can't believe they locked us up!" Don moaned. "Don't they understand it was just a mistake?"

The time dragged. I can't be sure just how much time, because our watches were with Don's napkin. It must have been at least a couple of hours. If we hadn't looked like criminals coming in, we must have by now — wild-eyed, nervous, sweaty, and disheveled.

Don sat on a small wooden chair, whistling "Ninety-nine Bottles of Beer on the Wall" through his teeth. I paced back and forth, wondering why it took so long to find out that the car was Joe's, and I was Jason, the address matched, and we were on the up-and-up.

Suddenly the door opened, and our cop escorted Ferguson into the room. The Peach had boosted our humiliation up to the next level by bringing Jessica along. It was a moment of perfect agony. Jessica's eyes were on me at last. Sure. Everybody wanted to get a look at the idiot who got arrested for stealing his own car. And what about Don? When the guy who moved in on your girl brings that girl to visit you in the slammer, it's a special kind of pain. I figured Don was going to grind Ferguson into a useless powder in front of every cop in town.

It didn't happen. Don's purple face and my red one both had the sense to keep their mouths shut.

The Peach, with his usual perfect logic, had straightened things out for the police in a way that no one else had thought of. He explained to them that they had Jason Cardone in custody for a car theft reported by Jason Cardone. It worked a lot better than what the cops were doing, which was trying to get in touch with the owner of the vehicle.

That meant Don and I could sign for our valuables and leave. "Don't forget to take our car off the hot sheet," I reminded the desk sergeant as I put on my watch and pocketed my wallet.

"Front pocket," Jessica reminded me.

Don was riffling through his pile of belongings with increasing agitation. "All right!" he bellowed. *"Who took my napkin?"*

"Relax, kid," said the desk sergeant. "We'll get you another napkin."

Don was red-faced. "But it *has* to be that one! Where is it?"

"A-choooo!"

We wheeled. Seated at a computer terminal, a constable, watery-eyed and sneezing, blew his nose into a large white —

"Napkin!" cried Don, wrenching the serviette away from the startled policeman's face. "It's *smeared*! Ah, but you can still read the number. . . ."

Jessica looked around the police station warily.

"I wonder how many of these people are *muggers*." Suddenly she pointed to a tall, bearded man in a black trenchcoat. "Officer!" she whispered urgently to the desk sergeant. "See that man over there?"

The sergeant whispered back, "What about him?"

"Don't you think it's funny he's wearing a long coat like that in the summer? Maybe he's hiding a sawed-off shotgun under there."

The sergeant stood up. "Probably not," he replied, and by now his whisper was loud enough for all to hear. "He's the police chaplain."

We hauled her out of there before she got us rearrested.

Rootbeer was waiting up, still squinting at his stamps. "So? How was it?"

"You're never going to believe this," I said. "We were in jail."

"Yeah, I know. The cops called here, asking about the car. They told me they were holding you, and I didn't want to spoil everything, so I hung up."

"*What?!*" I recalled our officer coming straight from the phone to lock us up. Now we knew why.

"Holding cells are so relaxing," the giant reminisced, a dreamy, far-off look in his eyes. "I've done some of my best meditation in jail. I warned Ferguson not to get you out too soon. You really need a good six or eight hours to — you know — gear down. I hope he didn't wreck it for you."

I stared at Rootbeer's earnest face. "No, it was just right," I said finally.

100

Seven

The fight that never happened happened the next morning. At the police station, Don had been hogtied. He couldn't yell at Ferguson for stealing his girl in front of said girl, nor could he go for the guy's throat in front of the cops. And Jessica was safe from his attack for her faithlessness not only because Don hadn't called her all week, but also because he held lovingly in his hand the telephone number of the beauteous Kiki. This left him only me to yell at, for forgetting to report that stolen car not stolen, which prompted me to offer to run him over with the aforementioned car.

"I can't believe you did this!" Don roared at the Peach, who was making things worse by being totally unruffled. "Haven't you ever heard of territory? You don't move in on another guy's girl!"

"I didn't," said Ferguson. "She asked me out."

"Aha!" Don was triumphant. "I caught you in a lie! And I can prove it! Jessica didn't have *my* number; I just had hers! So there's no way she could get in touch with you!"

"I was riding home in your uncle's limo, and we were stopped at a light, and I noticed Jessica waiting for the bus. It was raining, and I knew she lived around here, so I offered her a lift."

"That's even sleazier!" raged Don. "Using wealth and power to impress a girl! How low can you get?"

"Hey, hey, hey," interrupted Rootbeer. "Don't you guys know that arguments like this cause stress, and stress causes executive burnout?"

A "mind your own business" died on Don's lips. Rootbeer had been with us for a while, and all had been serene, but none of us ever lost sight of the fact that, at any moment, we could be on the receiving end of Bad Luck.

"You guys should take an interest in my stamp collection," the giant went on. "It really gets your mind off the pressures."

Don got his mind off Jessica by putting a call through to Kiki. It lasted about ten seconds.

"Her dad answered the phone," he told me. "What a bonehead that guy is."

"He didn't let you talk to her?" I asked.

"Worse than that. He said, 'There's no Kiki here.'"

"What are you going to do?"

Don shrugged. "Keep calling until *she* answers.

I'll try in the daytime, when he's at work."

Plotnick's voice came up through the vent. "If my daughter got phone calls from such a chrome polisher specialist like you, I'd commit suicide, kill myself, and then jump off a building."

"I'm feeling stress!" said Rootbeer warningly.

I thought there wasn't a man alive who wouldn't be intimidated by Rootbeer. I stand corrected. Plotnick could laugh off the neutron bomb if it wasn't going to cost him money.

"No wonder," he called back. "There's a lot of pressure in the gorilla business these days. You never know where your next banana is coming from."

I was excited. I couldn't wait for Rootbeer to go down there and rearrange some of Plotnick's lard. I would have helped, or at least called out suggestions. But Rootbeer just returned to his stamps. In his mammoth paws, he held up two tiny identical American stamps, depicting Thomas Jefferson.

"Hey, you've got two of that one," Don commented.

"The book says they're different," said Rootbeer, squinting his eyes into slits. "One's supposed to have ten and a half perforations, the other only ten." He began to count with an index finger three times the width of the stamp. "One, two, three, four — hold it, I think I missed that one. One, two, three — "

Suddenly he slammed the album shut hard enough to fuse the pages, and bellowed, "It's washday!"

In one lightning motion, he had the poncho over his head. An avalanche of stuff rained to the floor — an eggbeater, three pairs of sunglasses, one scuba flipper, a few crumpled bills and the odd coin, an Aztec fertility charm, a New Orleans city bus pass good for October 1981, an alarm clock with only one hand, a toilet brush, a mummified liverwurst sandwich, a Bulgarian-Greek pocket dictionary, a lime-green Nerf ball, and a diploma in the name of Gavin Gunhold from the University of Iowa. That was just the highlights. The pile was up to his knees, and things were still appearing. There were elastic bands and paper clips by the hundreds, a tangle of electrical wires, miles of string, wads of tape, random magnetic chess pieces, lint-covered raisins, and something that was either the Hope Diamond or a great big glass bottle stopper.

The three of us just stood there with our mouths hanging open as Rootbeer stepped out of the town dump, and proceeded to rip off the rest of his clothes, a sight that would make a summer all on its own. Then he filled up the tub, shook in half a box of Tide, and dumped all his clothes in. With the toilet brush (I wondered what that could be for) he pushed his laundry back and forth, like a witch stirring her brew. And by this time, the suds were on the ceiling. Then, satisfied that everything was moving along, he climbed into the tub himself, and began scrubbing his back with the toilet brush. (Why didn't I know that was coming?)

The phone rang. "Hello, darling." It was my mother. "Anything new?"

"It's washday."

* * *

Since I had to go get the newspaper anyway, for the Employment section, I was in charge of the shopping.

On Monday, I was in the grocery store, filling up my cart with our usual instant everything, when someone called my name. I looked up. There was Jessica, smiling and gesturing. Didn't it figure? I strut myself all over the neighborhood with absolutely no results, and now that I've finally written her off, guess who finds *me*?

"Am I ever glad to see you!" she said, waving a clipboard under my nose. "I'm totally confused."

"Well, first you have to get a cart — "

"No, no, I'm not shopping. This is an assignment for school."

I stared at her.

"Summer school," she said distastefully. "I flunked a course this spring, and my mom says I have to make it up."

"Yeah?" The wondrous Jessica got pushed around by her mom, too. How human of her! "What course?"

She looked ashamed. "Home ec."

"Home ec!?" I laughed in her face. It felt great. "How do you fail home ec?" Even Don had managed a D-minus in home ec.

She looked at me belligerently. "If you put salt instead of sugar in the soufflé, and you sew the waistband to the bottom of the apron instead of the top, and you set fire to your recipe book, you flunk." She shrugged sheepishly. "Especially if you cut a lot of classes, and forget to show up for the final exam." She showed me her clipboard, on

105

which she had written exactly one word: *Beans*.

"What's this?"

"My homework. It's a cost versus nutrition chart on at least twenty-five different products. You can help me."

What an honor! For this bright shining moment, I found myself wishing I had Plotnick's mouth. I mean, what had she done for *me* lately? All I said was, "Well, I'm kind of in a hurry to get home so I can start looking for a job — "

"This'll take two seconds!" she assured me, grabbing my arm and dragging me down the canned vegetables aisle.

Very quickly, I learned why Jessica had flunked home ec. She didn't know a pea from a carrot, and it was because she didn't want to know. I've never seen anybody care so little. I ended up doing the whole assignment.

When the chart was complete, I handed her the clipboard, and she looked at it in disgust. "This course is so stupid! What a waste of time!" was her comment.

I nodded in agreement. A waste of *my* time.

She glanced at her watch. "Oh, no! I'm late for class!" And she and her homework galloped off.

"You're welcome," I called sarcastically. But I was a coward. I waited until she was out of earshot.

An hour and a half behind schedule, I started the shopping. But it didn't go very well. Every time I picked up an item, I kept seeing it on Jessica's stupid chart. Our usual groceries were among the most expensive and the least nutritious items in the store. Maybe this home ec assignment wasn't so stupid after all. When you buy instant and prepared stuff, it costs a whole lot more than when you buy the ingredients and make it yourself. Plus instant food is full of tons of chemicals. In fact, when I checked all the labels on the stuff we'd been eating the last few weeks, there was monosodium glutamate and polysorbate 60 in every single thing!

So I got this brilliant idea. Instead of buying microwave chicken nuggets, I'd buy chicken; instead of TV dinners, I'd buy real food. And while saving a dollar or a dollar and a half here and there didn't seem like much, you've got to figure on three people eating three meals a day, each consisting of at least four or five elements — we could save twenty-five bucks a day! Seven hundred and fifty bucks a month! More, if you calculated it against Plotnick's deli prices! Maybe Jessica was going to get nothing out of her course, but to me it was the answer to our economic prayers.

Since the cash value was going to be enormous, I didn't feel bad about spending two hours filling my basket with exactly the right foods according to *The 90s Cookbook for the Woman on the Go*, which I bought, too. In fact, by the time I got all that stuff home, I realized that I'd forgotten to buy the paper. Oh well, at savings of $750 a month, job hunting could certainly wait until tomorrow. And I owed it all to that ingrate, Jessica Lincoln.

I didn't want to start off too fancy, so I figured I'd make hamburgers. Wouldn't you know it — there wasn't one word in that stupid useless cookbook about hamburgers. So I phoned the publisher. Turns out they wouldn't refund my money, but the lady talked me through her own recipe. I'd save time by cooking them up now and nuking them in the microwave at dinner. The problem was, I hadn't had lunch yet. So I ate mine for lunch, and I have to say it was great.

While I was working on a fourth burger to replace the one I'd eaten, Rootbeer came in and scarfed down the other two. Then I was out of ground beef. So we split the last burger, and I settled on roast chicken for dinner. The book said "Put the chicken in a 325° F oven and forget about it for two hours." That left me time to make soup. I couldn't wait to see the look on Ferguson's and Don's faces when they got home to find a meal fit for a king waiting for them.

I was slicing onions, and weeping delicately into a paper towel, when there was a loud buzz behind me. A small model World War I Fokker triplane whizzed past my ear, and landed with a resounding *kerplop* in the soup. I wheeled, and faced Rootbeer. There he stood in the center of the living room, remote control in hand, looking annoyed.

"What a place to put soup!"

"Sorry." Here I was, apologizing for preparing dinner in such a ridiculously unexpected location as the stove. Fear of Bad Luck does that to a person.

Rootbeer fished his plane out of the pot and licked the propeller experimentally. "Not bad. A little oily."

I examined the soup. It was a lot oily. "Rootbeer, what — ?" I indicated the Red Baron in his hands.

"I'm into model planes now. Stamp collecting isn't a real hobby. It gives you a headache."

I looked over to the corner, where the stamp albums now rested against the tripod, the boxes of

Kodak paper, and the developing chemicals. The camera was gone, probably to the pawnshop to finance the *Luftwaffe*.

Rootbeer placed the plane on the floor and manipulated the remote control. The engine spluttered, then labored, then died. He tried again. This time the propeller spun around a few times, the craft moved forward an inch or two, and *then* died. Try number three didn't yield a peep.

Rootbeer shook his head. "You go into something for relaxation, and you end up more stressed-out than before because they sell you a piece of garbage." With that, he stormed out of the apartment.

Dinner shaped up deliciously. The chicken was smelling great. The new pot of soup, sans motor oil, simmered on the stove, the salad was crisp and fresh and, as a special treat, I was baking a cake. It wasn't one of the top items on Jessica's chart. It was a D-Lishus chocolate fudge cake mix, but I hadn't been able to resist buying it.

I was about to put it in the oven when an unseen force took me over. When I was a little kid, my mother always used to make D-Lishus cakes. Being allowed to lick the spoon and scrape the bowl was the biggest thing in my life. D-Lishus cakes were pretty good, sure. But nothing was better than D-Lishus cake mix before it got baked. I always used to say that, if I had my way, that glorious stuff would never get near an oven. It was only my mother's presence that kept me from eating the whole thing. And today she was in Owen Sound. The real point of being on your own was getting to do stuff you normally couldn't.

I started with a tiny little bit on the end of my finger. It was ten times better than I remembered it. I found the biggest soup spoon in the place, and went to work. When the dust cleared, there was enough mix left for three cupcakes.

That's when the phone rang. It was Don. "I'm going to be working late tonight, Jason, so don't wait for me."

I was crushed. "But I cooked a great dinner!"

A crackle of laughter came through the receiver. "Yeah, right. Sure you did. See you later." Click.

It wasn't thirty seconds later that the phone rang again. Ferguson.

"Get your butt over here," I said. "Wait'll you see what I've made for dinner."

"I'm in New York," said the Peach.

"What? *Why?*"

"Mr. Robb needed me to meet some people from the U.S. operation. They want me to tour their plant, so I won't be back till late."

"But — but I've been slaving over a hot stove all day!"

"Sorry. Gotta go. I'll see you tonight."

I staggered back into the kitchen and stared at all that food, simmering, stewing, and cooling, and at the table, which really looked classy. I bellowed, *"Who's going to eat my dinner?"*

The door opened, and in stormed Rootbeer, muttering. "Stupid model planes — gotta be the stupidest hobby in the whole stupid world — hey, what smells so good?"

Rootbeer ate more than Don and Ferguson could have managed together, even if they'd both come home famished.

"You're a great cook, Jason! That was fantastic!"

"Thanks," I said, pleased. "Help me with the dishes?"

He said, "Sure thing," and went into Manchurian Bush Meditation, slipping off his chair with an enormous crash.

And as I washed up by myself, up to my ears in suds, it was the best thing about the meal that came back to me — the cupcakes. Well, not actually the finished product. I was going to have to get more of that mix! Fantastic!

Along with a snapshot of my brother Joe and Esmerelda on the beach somewhere in Spain, the mail brought a carrot cake from Mrs. Peach. It was a block of granite. God's Grandmother brought it up to us; don't ask me how. I'd have invited her in for a piece, but it would have shattered her dentures.

"Now I know why Peachfuzz loves Stonehenge so much," was Don's comment. "His mom baked it."

Don was irritable because Kiki's parents continued to insist there was no one by that name at that number. Around us, though, he played it cool.

"They can't keep her locked up forever," he said confidently. "Sooner or later, *she'll* answer the phone. Patience is the key."

I knew it was mostly an act, because he switched his chips back to Jessica, just in case. He was bouncing around the apartment, laughing and singing, when she agreed to go out with him Tuesday night.

"Eat your heart out, Peachfuzz! You've seen the

last of this chick! Friday night was temporary insanity! She's now fully recovered!"

Ferguson Peach must have ice water in his veins. He took it all — hours of bugging, insults, baiting, and sarcasm. But on Wednesday night, he went out for *his* date with Guess Who?

I was even more shocked than Don. Who did Jessica Lincoln think she was? Did she honestly believe there was nothing wrong with dating both my roommates at the same time? Eaten up with jealousy, I despised her. If there were a dozen people living in the apartment, instead of three, she'd probably be going out with eleven of them, leaving me high and dry! Stupid Jessica was having the summer of her life. And on top of it all, I had to referee the war between her two boyfriends.

"We should both dump her," growled Don. "She's playing head games with the two of us."

"You want to break up with her?" said Ferguson. "Be my guest."

"You'd like that, wouldn't you, Peachfuzz? Jessica all to yourself! Well, forget it! She's not going to you, even if I have to marry her, or kill her!"

All this was disturbing the fight against executive burnout. Rootbeer had taken up knitting, and had begun work on a pair of size twenty-three socks. If our large roommate got good and fed up with the bickering, and decided to hand out a little Bad Luck, who ended up with Jessica would no longer be an issue.

Don's next tactic was to soften Jessica up with a few gifts, mostly flowers and candy. Eventually he would be so *in* that, when he suggested she get rid of Ferguson, she would happily comply. This continued until one night Don caught Ferguson gift-wrapping a brass knuckles keychain.

"You call that a present?" howled Don, convulsed with laughter. "You're even stupider than I thought! Sure, go ahead! Give her to me on a silver platter!"

Wouldn't you know it — brass knuckles was just exactly what Jessica had always wanted. What good were flowers and candy and all the little luxuries if you couldn't protect yourself? (Her words, not mine.)

Things were getting tense. Don almost went so far as to join Jessica's *tae kwan do* class, but backed out when he found out that he had to wear the *gi*.

"There's no way I'm running around in public in a pair of pajamas, just for a *girl*!" he announced firmly. "And that's the name of that tune!"

The only person who didn't have a comment on the soap opera that was our lives was the one guy who normally stuck his nose into everything.

On Saturday morning, while Don put in some overtime at the car wash, Ferguson, Rootbeer, and I treated ourselves to breakfast in the deli. There we found Plotnick in a state of wild despair.

"Can you believe it?" he was raving. "That bum, that snake, that Hamish! Why him and not me?"

"What are you talking about, Mr. Plotnick?" asked Ferguson.

"You mean you haven't heard? You don't know? Sit down. No, you don't want breakfast. You'll throw up your guts when you hear this."

I sighed. "Okay, what happened to Hamish?"

"Hamish, who already has a fortune from gouging from his tenants and his customers, Hamish the parasite just got a $200,000 urban renewal grant from the city to help him buy more buildings and rob from more people." He shuddered. "Hamish is a rotten gangster, and to him comes $200,000. And what do I get? Plotnick, who slaves every day in the restaurant, and gives to charity, and is nice to everybody? For Hamish, money; for Plotnick, aggravation."

"What's to stop you from applying for one of those grants?" I asked.

"I have no interest in stealing from people," said Plotnick righteously.

"Actually," said Ferguson seriously, "to qualify for such a grant, you would have to invest in improving the neighborhood, which you are clearly unwilling to do — "

"Lies!" Plotnick interrupted. "Look how I renovated my staircase!"

"*We* renovated that staircase!" I exploded.

"Could I please have some coffee?" Rootbeer asked politely.

Plotnick cast him a burning look. "Shouldn't you be out volunteering for scientific experiments?"

"No offense, Mr. Plotnick, but please lay off," I said. "Lose yourself in your work. If you sell enough coffee, you'll have as much money as Hamish."

Plotnick waddled off in the direction of the counter. "Listen to him, the President of the Stock Exchange, a layabout too lazy to get an honest job, he's got something to say."

"Hey!" I howled. "I'm looking for a job!"

"Oh, yeah? How many interviews did you go

on this week, Mr. Cardone? Five? Ten? None, maybe?"

"Listen!" I seethed. "I've been cooking, and cleaning, and shopping, and that's important stuff! A house doesn't run itself, you know — " What was I saying? This was my mother's speech, right down to the tone of voice. I stopped before I got to the part about how unappreciated I was.

As Plotnick brought the coffee, Don burst in, wild-eyed. He stomped up to our booth and sat down so loudly I'm positive he must have fractured his *derriere*. None of us said anything, so he stood up again and bellowed, "Well, if you *must* know, I lost my job!"

"Good idea," approved Rootbeer. "If you don't love what you do, don't do anything."

Plotnick placed cups in front of the three of us. "Coffee for Mr. Champion the loser?"

"Leave him alone!" I exploded.

"Yeah, sure," Don told our landlord. He slumped down again, resting his head on top of his arms like grade-school kids do when the student who stole a book or something is given a chance to return it without being seen. From down there, he told us what had happened.

"This moronic rich kid is showing off for his girlfriend by making me polish all the chrome a thousand times. And she's giggling away like an idiot, thinking he's the cleverest guy in the world. So he tells me to do the hubcaps again — he can't even see the dumb hubcaps. I say they're fine, he says do them anyway so I wax up my cloth with the polishing gunk, and throw it right in his face!"

"Aw, Don," I groaned.

"You know what your problem is, Mr. Champion?" called Plotnick from behind the counter. "You don't know your place. You're a nobody. You should have said, 'Sure, mister, I'll polish your hubcaps.' "

"And let him get away with it?" Don challenged.

Plotnick brought Don his cup. "Dummy! When you're down there scrubbing, you let the air out of his tires, the *shtunk*! No one can prove it was you. So you keep your job, and on the first of the month, when your landlord, such a nice man, asks for the rent, you have it."

"Did you get the license number?" inquired Rootbeer. "I'll bet we could track him down, and then maybe he'd have some *bad luck*."

"No!" I blurted out. "I mean, no thanks, Rootbeer." To Don I added, "Don't worry. You'll find something else."

"Big talk from the unemployment line," piped Plotnick, his spirits improving.

Rootbeer was going on about the joys of not having a job. "When cash gets tight, you can always pick up a few bucks here and there."

"Rootbeer," I said, "not everybody has a stomach that can withstand a two-by-four."

"Okay," said the giant thoughtfully. "Could you handle maybe a brick dropped on your head?" He snapped his fingers. "I once made five hundred bucks just for eating twenty-six pounds of bananas."

"Did you get sick?"

"Oh, yeah," said Rootbeer. "But when I came out of the bathroom three days later, the money was still there."

116

"The part that bums me out," Don said, "is where am I going to get some cash to take out Jessica?"

"I can spot you a few bucks," said Ferguson generously.

Don snorted. "That's not funny."

But the Peach was sincere. "No, really."

Don's eyes narrowed. "What's your game, Peachfuzz? You're trying to come off as the big father figure — 'oh, here's a quarter, sonny, go get yourself an ice cream cone.' Then, before I know it, you're using it against me with Jessica. It's all tactics. Well, forget it. There are plenty of inexpensive places a guy can take a girl."

"Sure!" I enthused. "The park, the botanical gardens, the museum; you can have conversations, get to know each other — "

Don made a face. "Maybe I'll tell her I've got the mumps."

Eight

That rotten Plotnick would never again be able to say *I* wasn't looking for work. I had an interview for a busboy job at a downtown family restaurant, and I could just feel that today was my day. The guy on the phone sounded really impressed with my personality.

I put on my best slacks, and a clean white shirt, and was giving myself a last once-over in the mirror when there was a knock at the door. I opened it up to reveal the last person on earth I wanted to see — Jessica Lincoln. She was carrying two large shopping bags, and smiling with all thirty-two teeth.

"They're both out," I said coolly. Ferguson was

at work, and Don was pounding the pavement.

Undaunted, she pushed past me into the apartment, and set the bags down on the kitchen counter.

"Oh, Jason, I'm in big trouble!" she greeted me. "If I don't have a casserole by eleven o'clock, I'm finished!"

"So make one," I said indifferently.

Her warped mind interpreted this as my offer to help. She began to unpack the bags. "Thanks, Jason! I knew I could count on you! Now, I bought all the ingredients — at least, I think I did — "

"Wait a minute," I interrupted her. "You'll have to do this at home. I've got an interview."

"I picked the fastest casserole," she said briskly. "Mexican Taco. It'll only take two seconds."

Disgusted, I looked at my watch. Fortunately I'd left plenty of time to get to my interview. If this was really a fast casserole, I could oblige this pain in the butt, and still make it downtown by ten-thirty.

I joined her in the unpacking. "I don't see why you don't ask Don or Ferguson to do this stuff," I muttered sarcastically.

She didn't get the point. "Oh, can they cook?"

She was totally inept. She had the wrong kind of flour, pepper instead of peppers, and where the recipe called for tabasco, she'd bought tobacco — the chewing kind that baseball players wad into their cheeks.

Her total participation in this makeshift casserole (don't worry, I didn't use the tobacco) consisted of looking over my shoulder while I chopped, stirred, and improvised. Not that I was such a great cook. But at least I could follow a few simple instructions. When it came to home ec, Jessica had a fifteen-second attention span. She'd be watching me one minute, staring at the ceiling the next, and before long the TV would be on.

Finally the casserole was in the oven. I sent Jessica to the store to pick up some corn chips to decorate the top, and I went to change my shirt, which was spattered and sweat-soaked. It was going to take a mad dash downtown to get me to my interview on time, but I would make it. I stepped into the bathroom for some last-minute grooming.

I heard Jessica come back, and called to her, "Take it out of the oven. It's ready."

Two minutes later, a voice that was definitely not Jessica's said, "Thanks a lot, Jason. It was delicious."

I burst out of the bathroom and arrived in the kitchen at the same instant that Jessica returned with the corn chips. There sat the casserole dish, completely empty. Rootbeer stood over it, pulling stray tendrils of cheese out of his shaggy beard. Jessica's project had gone straight out of the oven and down the hatch.

"My homework!" she wailed.

"Aw, Rootbeer," I moaned, "why'd you eat the casserole?"

He was mystified. "You said it was ready."

"I meant ready to come out of the oven! Jessica needed it for her home ec class!"

Rootbeer looked contrite. "I can maybe go to school with her and tell them how great it was. Although it could have used a little tabasco."

"No!" cried Jessica.

"Okay, I'll leave out the part about the tabasco." She was so upset that he added, "Well, could you maybe make another one?"

She consulted her watch. "There's still time — "

"Not for me," I said firmly. "I've got to leave right now."

But her distress halted my progress for the door — that and Rootbeer's plea.

"Aw, come on, Jason," coaxed the giant. Then he belched, and for some reason I felt that the whole misunderstanding was, in a way, my fault. After all, it had been I who spoke the fatal words, "It's ready."

"All right," I sighed. "Wash the dish. We'll start over."

"Oh, Jason, you're wonderful!" Jessica breathed.

"Yeah, yeah, tell me about it."

In celebration, Rootbeer keeled over into Manchurian Bush Meditation.

Jessica jumped back in shock. "The casserole! We poisoned him!"

"Good. Let's make another one, and we can poison your whole class," I said, gathering the ingredients.

By the time I shipped Jessica off to school with the new casserole, ten-thirty had come and gone, along with my interview. I phoned to reschedule, but the job was already taken. Just another grievance to chalk up to Jessica's account.

I figured there must be hundreds of family restaurants in Toronto, so I started phoning out of the Yellow Pages in search of one in need of a busboy

121

(who could double as a casserole chef). Soon, though, my mind started to wander, and I found myself pacing around between calls, turning the TV on and off.

In a blinding flash, I recognized the symptoms. It was just like Jessica and her home ec. I hated looking for a job so much that I could only do it when I absolutely forced myself, and even then, for only two or three minutes at a stretch. For the first time, I felt sorry for her, having to sit in a hot classroom two hours a day, learning about something that interested her absolutely zero.

Well, at least she had a casserole to hand in. If it wasn't for me, she'd be the only person in the history of high school to fail home ec *twice* — including summer school, where they give you points for spelling your name right. The grade she got on this project would probably carry her through the whole course.

Or would it? How did *I* know I'd get an A on that casserole? It wasn't like I was one of the great chefs of Europe. The only person besides me who had ever eaten my cooking was Rootbeer, and you couldn't go by him. Rootbeer would eat a bus if it slowed down in front of him. What if my casserole got a lousy mark?

I stood up and started pacing around the room. What did I care? If she flunked, it would be no more than she deserved. Without so much as a cooking lesson, under time pressure, and with the wrong ingredients, I had come up with a casserole. That was an accomplishment, no matter what grade I got. Besides, surely it was worth at least a B. A C?

I made a few more calls, but I was watching the clock like crazy. At five to one, I could bear it no longer. The job search would just have to wait until I found out how I was doing in home ec. I ran out to Bathurst Street, hoping to intercept Jessica on her way home from school. Since I didn't know her address or telephone number, I had to catch her here, or wait to find out through whichever of my roommates had a date with her tonight. I wouldn't be able to stand the hours of not knowing!

Then I spotted her, across the street, down the road, climbing up the front steps of her house. I put on the afterburners to catch up, and got there just as she was opening her door. I reached out and tapped her on the shoulder.

"Hey, how'd — ?"

She pivoted like a prizefighter and bashed me one in the face with her brass knuckles keychain. It wasn't a very hard punch, and thank God for that, because I caught all metal. I went down heavily, seeing stars. I tried to call her off, but in my haze, I couldn't put the ideas together. So I struggled to get up. But she'd already grabbed an aerosol can from her belt, and I was getting a snootful of hair spray. A loud, piercing siren cut the air, emanating from a small black box in her free hand. Then, and only then, did she look down at her victim.

"Oh, my God! Jason! I'm so sorry!" She hustled me upstairs and pushed me into the kitchen, which was at the front of the apartment. "I feel so bad!" she said. "It's just that, when you reached for me, I thought my number was up."

"I felt the same way," I said, "only it turned out to be true."

She got most of the blood off my face, but you could just see where the shiner was going to swell up and blacken.

She shook her head sadly. "*This* is the result of a city that's filled with crime!"

No. This was the result of getting punched in the face by an idiot with a brass knuckles keychain. I was more convinced than ever that the day I met Jessica Lincoln was the worst day of my entire life.

I was in such a hurry to get out of there that I almost forgot the reason for this fatal visit. I paused on the porch, and asked about my casserole.

"Oh, it was great!" she enthused. "I got an A." And she slammed the door in my face.

"You're welcome," I told it.

My black eye turned 1 Pitt Street into a hospital. I started out in God's Grandmother's apartment with an application of ice. Then Wayne Gretzky's Sister ran in with the perfect ointment. The Ugly Man advised me to prepare myself for excruciating pain. When I finally got back to the second floor, the Stripper was waiting for me. She had overheard the various conversations through the ventilation duct, and was positive I was receiving inadequate care. *Heat*, not cold, should be used to reduce swelling. This was loudly applauded by the Phantom through his closed door.

Even Plotnick got into the act. He sent up a bowl of chicken soup, along with a bill for $1.75.

I got sympathy in apartment 2C, too, especially from Don, who was the last to arrive. "Jason!" he

whispered at the sight of me. "You didn't have —
Bad Luck!?"

I glared at him accusingly. "It was your woman
who did it. I highly recommend that you never
come up on her from behind." Then to Ferguson,
"Some *idiot* gave her a souvenir keychain from
Murder Incorporated!"

"A girl did this?" said Rootbeer, impressed. "Got
her phone number?"

"She's with me," said Don.

"On her off-days," Ferguson conceded.

"You're about to have an off-day, Peachfuzz!"
growled Don. "It starts with my fist, and ends in
the cemetery!"

And they were at it again, bickering back and
forth over who should get the girl and who should
bow out.

My eye throbbing, I went to the bathroom to
refill the Stripper's hot water bottle. How come the
people with the least to complain about end up
doing all the whining?

"So we drive to this sleazy bar that's attached to
this gas station, and inside it's all truckers, and
Rootbeer points to this humungous truck tire on
the wall, and goes, *'Twenty bucks says Old Puncture
Proof can't last thirty seconds with me!'* "

It was Monday morning, and the three of us were
having breakfast in the deli. Don had been Rootbeer Racinette's assistant in last night's "work." He
had gone along at Rootbeer's insistence. Our giant
roommate felt he could draw extra inspiration and
strength from someone who had so recently lost
his job.

125

"The whole bar goes nuts, and all these truckers are breaking their arms handing over twenties, and babbling about how they've driven over broken glass, and nails, and diamond drill bits with that brand of tire, and never had a flat. So they get Old Puncture Proof down off the wall and roll it out to the gas station — it's taller than we are, and I'm freaking out because there are, like, thirty of them, and only two of us. And there's no way anybody could burst that tire with a bazooka, let alone bare hands. Jason, you're not going to believe it!"

"The kitchen's packed with groceries, so we'll have to believe it," said Ferguson.

"Who asked you?" retorted Don. He turned back to me. "They fill up the tire from the air hose, and Rootbeer cleans this little patch with windshield washer fluid. I'm wondering what's he going to do. Punch it? Stomp on it? Stick his fingers in the treads and rip it apart? Check this out! He opens his mouth and *bites* the tire!"

"Get out of here!" I blurted.

"*Pow!* The inner tube pops instantly, and before you know it, Old Puncture Proof is flat as a pancake, and there's Rootbeer, spitting rubber and smiling. Jason, I missed the age of the dinosaurs, but now I know what it must have been like to watch Tyrannosaurus rex lean over and take a chunk out of some poor Apatosaurus!"

"Actually," said the Peach, "the Apatosaurus and most of the other sauropods were already extinct by the late Cretaceous period when Tyrannosaurus rex began to appear."

"Well, even so, it was still amazing," asserted Don.

"I should think you'd be impressed by that kind of degenerate behavior, Mr. Champion," called Plotnick from the counter. "An unemployed houseguest of a street fighter who comes home bruised and bloody all the time."

"It happened *once*, Mr. Plotnick! And it was an accident!" I snapped. Plotnick had been on me all weekend. Most of the swelling was down, but I still had a technicolor face. I turned back to Don. "And Rootbeer screamed all the way home, right?"

"Not really. But he couldn't talk. We pulled into a 7-11 and I bought him a bag of ice. He bit into it, and we sat there for a while. I think I got to know him better — you know — from the human side."

"You mean the gorilla side," put in Plotnick, filling up our cups. "You know, gentlemen, you could make a lot of money from Mr. Racinette. Just phone up the museum and tell them you've found the Missing Link."

I frowned at our landlord. "You don't like anybody, do you?"

He looked at me severely. "The persons I like, Mr. Cardone, don't cause any hassles, or break into buildings and cars, or go around eating tires and dropping dead all the time. Now I've got three persons and one gorilla all living in a one-person apartment, paying less rent than that criminal Hamish gets for something a quarter the size. And this is supposed to make me love all mankind? Phooey!" He waddled over to another booth, where Romeo and Juliet were enjoying a romantic breakfast. "Hey, you — break it up!"

The Peach rose. "Well, I've got to get going. I'll probably be late. We've got some efficiency experts from Tokyo coming up to evaluate my new improved production line."

Don held his head. "Now they're coming from Japan to look at his fuzz-brained ideas! Where next? The moon? How'd he get to be so *smart*? He can't even skate!"

I laughed. "I always knew he had *something*. I just didn't think anybody would ever have any use for it, that's all."

Because of my black eye, I had to suspend the job search. Outwardly I complained bitterly, but I was rejoicing on the inside. While Don scoured the city for a job, I went to the beach, toured museums and art galleries, went to the movies, and even took the Camaro for a spin to Niagara Falls.

"It doesn't seem fair," Don grumbled. "I'm busting my butt, and you're on vacation."

"It's my eye," I explained. "Who'd hire me with a face like this? You heard Plotnick. I look like a brawler."

Don snorted. "You can hardly see it anymore."

"Look," I said defensively, "did I ask your woman to throw me the k.o. punch? As soon as I'm back to normal, I'll be right out there with you."

The bruise continued to fade. I actually toyed with the idea of enhancing it a little with mascara. I knew the Stripper was a makeup expert. Maybe she'd help me.

But then Don got hired on as a stock boy at a publishing company, and the jig was up. The next morning, Jason Cardone was once again looking for a job.

Almost immediately, my mind started playing the usual tricks on me. A little dust here, a rumpled sheet there, anything to keep me away from that phone. Then I started cooking again. During the black eye, I hadn't felt the *slightest urge* to turn on the stove! I started with dinner, but soon an elaborate luncheon became a habit, too. I began preparing brown bag lunches for Ferguson and Don. I told them it was because I felt bad about not contributing to the expenses. But the real reason was that, by preparing them the previous afternoons, I could use up even more job-hunting time.

Then I diversified into laundry. It was a godsend. Laundry takes *hours*.

What was the matter with me? There was a time back in Owen Sound when my bed didn't get made from one month to the next. Why was the sight of a rumpled sheet suddenly so intolerable? Cooking, cleaning, washing, ironing — these used to be nothing more than dirty words in my mother's list of Things to Nag About Today. Now not only did I do them — they were my whole life!

Was I goofing off? No way! There wasn't a job on earth that would have me working this hard! I couldn't believe maintaining one little apartment could be so complicated. Could you imagine a whole house? Talk about a no-win situation! You wash clothes — somebody wears them; you make beds — somebody sleeps in them; the more you cook, the more dishes you have to scrub. All your accomplishments reset to zero. It's discouraging.

And it doesn't help when your roommates are such slobs. Don and Ferguson made a mess, but Rootbeer *was* a mess, looking for a place to strew itself. At the rate he was going, pretty soon the debris from his old abandoned hobbies would be challenging the rest of us for breathing space. The knitting stuff was there in the corner now, too, along with the shortest-lived hobby of all — Parcheesi. (There are no Parcheesi leagues in Toronto.)

One day I got the bright idea to rearrange some of the furniture. But the problem was that the section under where the couch used to be was cleaner than the rest of the carpet. So I had to shampoo the rug, which made everything else in the apartment look lousy, so I had to vacuum the upholstery, wax the floor, and wash the walls. I barely had time to make dinner.

Ferguson and Don hardly noticed the change in me. Between overtime and Jessica, they weren't around much, and rarely showed up for dinner. No matter what I said or did, those insensitive clods just made fun of me anyway.

"I thought we came to Toronto to get away from our mothers," was Ferguson's comment.

Don put it more succinctly. "Get off my back." Or sometimes he just laughed and laughed until I wanted to kill him.

I didn't have a hope of domesticating them, but it wasn't much of a hard sell becoming the personal chef of Rootbeer Racinette. He always came and went on a pretty erratic schedule, but lately he'd been showing up at noon and six like clockwork. We even had a favorite dessert — D-Lishus chocolate fudge cake mix (uncooked) with whipped cream and strawberries. I didn't tell him what it was. I called it "Cardone Surprise." I was even managing to ease a little dishwashing into his routine, although when I pushed him too far, he'd be flopped on the floor, meditating, in the wink of an eye.

Fatness was becoming an imminent danger — not for Rootbeer, whose sheer size went beyond such classifications, but for me. All that tasting, eating, and Cardone Surprise was beginning to fill out my clothes alarmingly. So I began each day with a two-mile run around the neighborhood. At first, I used to pick up a newspaper for the job hunt. But sweating off all the Cardone Surprise could reduce *The Toronto Star* to papier-mâché in seconds.

And the first day I jogged up to apartment 2C without the Employment section under my arm was when I knew in my heart what I refused to accept and still don't understand: I had become a sixteen-year-old house husband.

"Excuse me, sir, I know you don't approve of me," Don was saying into the pay phone in the deli, "but Kiki and I would really like to see each other . . . well, I know she lives there because this is the number she gave me. . . . I don't think there's any reason to use that kind of language . . ." He shot us a pained look. "He hung up again! What a Nazi!"

We were having dinner in the deli Friday night. The one day I hadn't bothered to cook, both those idiots showed up after work right on time. I guess Miss Lincoln, ace party girl, home ec failure, and heavyweight champion was taking a breather.

"Love never comes easy," said Romeo sympathetically as Don passed by on his way to our booth.

"You know, Don," I suggested carefully, "maybe it really *is* the wrong number. After all, the napkin got pretty smeared up."

"It's plain as anything," said Don. "And it's the right number. You think a great girl like Kiki doesn't know her own phone number?"

Ferguson had another explanation. "Maybe she deliberately gave you the wrong number."

"I realize that's *your* experience, Peachfuzz," said Don acidly, "but no one ever does that to *me*. Besides, there's no doubt in my mind that this is her father I'm talking to. He's got a voice to match his face — sour pickles."

"A man of taste," came Plotnick's voice from the kitchen.

Don's outlook was generally pretty bleak lately. Besides his telephone problems, and the fact that he still hadn't convinced Jessica to dump Ferguson, his new job with the publishing company was physically exhausting.

"Oh, it's a barrel of laughs," he said sarcastically. "Check this out. A truck filled with ten-thousand-pound crates pulls up, and I lift all the ten-thousand-pound crates down and put 'em in the warehouse. Then I take a different pile of ten-thousand-pound crates from the warehouse, and throw 'em on the truck. Then we have a little cardiac resuscitation, but not for too long, because there's another truck waiting."

"They must sell a lot of books," I commented lamely.

"Tell me about it. They've got a best-seller. A social studies textbook for kindergarten kids. I read it yesterday on agony break. It says kindergarten is a society, so everybody has to share their toys. $18.95." He sighed. "It's not much fun, but at least the pay is bad."

"I got a promotion," said Ferguson shyly.

Don glared at him. "What are you now — king?"

Plotnick placed three sandwiches in front of us. "They're robbing you blind, Mr. Peach! You're making sewer cleaner money for a big fancy job!"

Ferguson was unconcerned. "I'm up another fifty a week. And besides, I enjoy what I'm doing."

"Good boy," approved God's Grandmother from her stool at the counter. "Money isn't everything."

Plotnick threw his arms in the air. "I'm surrounded by crazy people! Oi, here comes the gorilla."

We all looked out the show window to see Rootbeer lumbering up the street, lugging a huge, awkward package. Spying us, the giant waved cheerfully, opened the door, and stuffed himself and his burden inside.

"You took unto yourself a bride, Mr. Racinette?" quipped Plotnick, pointing at the package with his meat fork.

Rootbeer set it down with a thud, and there was a strange, vibrant ringing in the deli, sort of like the sound you hear just before the alien spaceship lands in movies they play at five A.M. on TV.

"I bought a harp," he announced delightedly.

I was appalled. "A *what*?"

"A harp." Eagerly he ripped off the brown paper

133

to uncover a full-size forty-six-string harp, elaborately carved, and painted gold. "Listen to this sound!" He began running sausagelike fingers back and forth across the strings.

"I'm dead!" cried Plotnick. "I can hear the angel music!"

"Where you're going, they don't have harps; they have barbecue pits," the Peach shot back.

"Mr. Peach, on the scale of annoying between 1 and 10, you're at least a 12."

"It's my new hobby," Rootbeer told us all. "Isn't it great?"

Our landlord was unimpressed. "One noise complaint, Mr. Cardone, and you, and your houseguests, and your musical gorilla are *out*!" He turned to Rootbeer. "So what do you want to order?"

"Your execution," I said feelingly.

Ferguson was looking at the evening paper. "Hey, Mr. Plotnick, your friend Hamish has a big ad in the Entertainment section. The Pop Bistro's bringing in a guest chef from Paris, and next week is Gourmet Week."

Plotnick turned gray in the face. "Thank you, Mr. Peach, for reminding everybody of Plotnick's favorite subject. That skunk, that weasel, that racketeer, has come up with another fancy way to rob people. What can you get from his restaurant that you can't get from mine?"

"Food," all three of us chorused without hesitation.

"Three comedians in my restaurant." The dangerous stabbing movement of the meat fork belied Plotnick's beaming expression. "So if my food is so terrible, why don't you go over to Hamish and

134

throw up your guts while your pocket is being picked?"

"We tried that," said Don in annoyance, "but some loudmouth told them not to let us in."

"I look after my tenants," said our landlord piously. "What would have happened if the police had come by checking up?"

"They do that?" I asked.

"Of course. I would have phoned them myself. Besides, Mr. Cardone, your brother, also Mr. Cardone, told me to keep an eye on you. And when he comes back, boy, am I going to have stories to tell!"

Nine

Gourmet Week at the Pop Bistro was a resounding success. Suddenly our seedy little neighborhood was the hottest place in town, just as we'd envisioned in the pre-summer buildup. Cars, even a few limos, were double-parked on Bathurst and all the side streets, Pitt included, and customers lined up around the block to get into Hamish's restaurant. It was wonderful, mostly because it was driving Plotnick insane.

"I can't stand it! It's more than a person can bear!" The mere mention of Gourmet Week brought out the veins in our landlord's bald head. He sat like a stone behind the counter, unable to provide table service. "He charges $6 for a lousy bowl of soup; he charges $20 for a millionth of a chicken, it wouldn't make a meal for an ant; he charges $10 just to walk in the door and listen to that terrible music! He's a criminal! He should be put in the electric chair!"

I suspended cooking, just so we wouldn't miss the sight of our beloved landlord brought to his knees. We ate all our meals in the deli, serving ourselves. And whenever we could, we made sure to remind Plotnick that business was still booming down the street for good old Hamish.

By Wednesday, he could take it no longer. I was pouring myself some more coffee at dinner when I overheard him disguising his voice on the kitchen phone.

"I just had supper at that miserable Pop Bistro, and there was a cockroach in my food as big as a Volkswagen. You're the Board of Health. Do something about it — " Then in the normal voice, "Go and sit down and mind your own business, Mr. Cardone. And don't be so generous with my coffee. You think it grows on trees?"

Then he switched to anonymous calls to the police, tipping them off to the many illegally parked vehicles in the neighborhood. Soon tow trucks were everywhere, hauling away the cars of Hamish's customers. To Plotnick's dismay, the stream of patrons didn't falter.

We were really enjoying our landlord's misery until, on Thursday night, I glanced from his morose face out the window to the crowded street. My eyes fell on the Camaro. It was rising, hind end first, above the row of parked vehicles.

"What the — ?"

Then I saw the tow truck. It had the logo of the Metropolitan Toronto Police on it, and it was signaling left to pull out and take away *my car*!

"Hey!" I was up and out of the booth like a shot. As I rocketed out the door, I caught a lopsided smile from Plotnick, his first all week.

"Was that *your* car, Mr. Cardone?"

I saved my breath for the road race against the tow truck — fourteen blocks, uphill most of the way. I was fuming. From his spot behind the counter, that rotten Plotnick must have had a perfect view of Joe's car being cranked up and hauled away. But he'd never said a word of warning.

A last-ditch sprint caught me up with the truck as it waited its turn to enter the expressway. I couldn't speak, so I banged on the window and hyperventilated. The Camaro was hanging there, a lopsided aerodynamic black hole. Why me?

The driver rolled down the window. "Yeah?"

"Sir! Mister! (gasp) Mister! (gasp) Hold it! You can't tow away that car! (gasp) That's a (gasp) legal parking space!"

He looked down at me. "This your car?"

"Yeah! And it was *legally parked*!"

He examined a clipboard and shrugged. "It's on my pickup list. You steal it?"

I gulped loudly. Oh, no. Joe's car was still on the hot sheet. That desk sergeant had forgotten to take it off, after I'd specifically reminded him to.

It took half the night to get the car out of the police garage.

"Don't you know it's Gourmet Week?" asked the sergeant on duty.

"Look," I said, biting back rage, "this is the second time you've impounded my car. *Please* take it off the stolen list."

"Of course. That happens automatically."

"But it *didn't* happen!"

The man manipulated the computer terminal in front of him. "Look, kid, I'm doing it right now. I promise you, your troubles are over."

I had to be satisfied with that. But I was far from satisfied with our dear landlord. When I brought the Camaro home close to midnight, I had revenge in my heart.

"Man," I seethed, "I was prepared for the big city, but nothing can prepare a guy for anything like Plotnick! He took our money and rebuilt his whole staircase, he fixed it so we couldn't get into the Pop Bistro, he tries to rip us off, he threatens to kick us out, he dumps all over everything we try to do, he calls us names, he's always spying on us and minding our business, and now it's his fault the Camaro got towed away, just because he's jealous of that Hamish guy! Boy, I'd like to get even!"

"Shhh!" Ferguson put his finger to his lips and pointed at the air vent. He unfolded himself from the beanbag chair, and turned on the stereo, loud. Then he beckoned us to a meeting in the kitchen, the furthest place in the whole apartment from the vent that was Plotnick's communication system. "I have an idea."

"You're crazy!" whispered Don. "Revenge on Plotnick? We touch one brick of his precious building, and he'll put up the Taj Mahal and slap it on our tab!"

"Besides," I added, "he's holding Joe's lease over our heads. If we lose this apartment, we're dead meat."

"It's nothing like that," said the Peach, his eyes taking on the gleam that indicated one of his weirder moods. "This won't hurt Plotnick *or* the building. Listen."

Hey, this was the guy who was single-handedly leading Plastics Unlimited into the twenty-first century. We were all ears.

Friday our dinner consisted of Burger King take-out. We ate it in a tiny alley on Bathurst Street, sandwiched between a pawnshop and a twenty-four-hour dry cleaner. We were on stake-out. We had a good view of the deli, and also of the giant pot hole on Bathurst. With all the traffic to Gourmet Week, there had to be at least one car that would hit at the right angle, at the right speed, and donate its hubcap to our cause.

We were lucky. It took just about an hour. At exactly seven thirty-nine, we heard the squeal of tires. We all stiffened at the sound, and I pictured Plotnick behind the counter, doing the same. A big black Ford roared up the street and hit the pot hole full tilt. We couldn't have asked for a hubcap with more momentum. It was spinning like a flying saucer, hurtling towards the deli.

I pictured Plotnick again. He was on the alert! He would reach for his trusty butterfly net! But he couldn't pick it up! *It was Krazy-glued to the side of the counter!* He would panic! He would scream! I'd been wondering all day what words would pass his lips while he watched at least $20.00 worth of potential income hit the pavement, becoming dented and unsaleable, and therefore getting away.

"My window!"

His window?

"Oh, my God!" cried Don. "He's coming out!"

Waddling at top speed, Plotnick bravely went to face the hubcap unarmed. He interposed his portly body between the spinning projectile and the plate glass window. It was a case of "your money or your life," and Plotnick was making the obvious choice.

The hubcap hit the curb at top speed, and bounced up at a forty-five degree angle. It caromed off Plotnick's bald head, and crashed through the showcase window of the Olympiad Delicatessen. Neatly it severed the string of salamis, which dropped like torpedoes to the glass-covered floor. Neighbors and customers swarmed around the fallen restaurateur.

Plotnick was okay, according to the doctor who made the house call. For once, the ventilation system worked in our favor. We heard everything. There was no concussion, just a little bruise that would fade in a few days. Apparently he was as hardheaded as he was hard-hearted.

The post-revenge victory party that night in apartment 2C was subdued. We had the stereo cranked way up — that was just sound interference so Plotnick couldn't listen in. After all, a window had been broken today, and if he found out it was us, pretty soon there'd be a ninety-story office tower at 1 Pitt Street, and we'd have to pay for it.

We were listening to a tape of Rootbeer on the

harp, made for our "enjoyment." People normally think of the harp as a quiet instrument. But that reverberating *plink, plink* gets inside your guts and vibrates them. Maybe Rootbeer was avoiding executive burnout, but the rest of us were going crazy.

"Look," said Ferguson, "Plotnick's okay, so all he's lost is a window — which was rotten of us, but we didn't do it on purpose. And the money he has to spend to fix it he's already extorted from us when he re-did the stairs. So we're even."

I nodded. "Plotnick's earned everything he gets, and more. But I feel like I took that hubcap, hit him over the head with it, and tossed it through his window. Bashing stuff up is almost — vandalism. You can't get much lower than that." I winced. "We deserve this music."

"I wouldn't go that far," said Ferguson.

"I enjoyed every minute of it," announced Don. "Not because of Plotnick's head or the window, but because Peachfuzz thought it up, planned the whole thing, and it *didn't work*. I mean, if this hadn't happened, we might never have lived to see his Royal Fuzziness mess up."

"You're not going to let me forget this, are you?" said the Peach.

"Absolutely not," Don beamed. "Let it be known to one and all that, on this date, A.D. 1990, at approximately twenty minutes to eight P.M., in the city of Toronto, country of Canada, continent of North America, planet Earth, orbit 3, solar system 60609, the great Doctor of Fuzzology made a *mistake*. Every year, on this anniversary, expect to hear from me, Peachfuzz, to remind you that the guys who built Stonehenge never would have screwed up like this!"

"Blessed events aside," I cut in, "I feel pretty lousy about it."

"Revenge is overrated," agreed Ferguson.

We felt so guilty that, when the tape ended, we almost played it again. Almost. Instead, we huddled around the air vent, listening for sounds from the deli. Plotnick seemed to be his normal nasty self. But when the man from the twenty-four-hour glass replacement company told him the new window would cost $330, he hit the ceiling. We felt like murderers.

"We'll give him the money," I said suddenly.

"You mean confess?" gasped Don.

"Of course not. We'll just put three hundred and thirty bucks in an envelope, and slide it under his door after he's gone to sleep. He'll never know who did it." I turned to the Peach. "You cashed your paycheck, right?"

"Giving him money goes against the grain," said Ferguson, nodding sadly. "You know he'll get it all anyway, so why speed the process?"

"Plotnick doesn't deserve two cents," I acknowledged, "but our consciences are worth more than three hundred and thirty bucks."

"To see Peachfuzz make a mistake," grinned Don, "I'd gladly hand over a million!"

With our consciences clear, we slept till almost noon. Then we headed down to the deli to eat à la Plotnick. After all, we'd prepaid the tip, $330, at five o'clock in the morning.

Suddenly Plotnick was all smiles, and the nickel-sized bruise on his forehead looked more like a Bozo-the-Clown polka dot than a wound. He was laughing and joking with his customers, and full table service was restored, in spite of the fact that Gourmet Week still had one big night to go. The new window was already installed, spotless and gleaming. We all looked our fill. Not only was it ours, but this was also probably the only chance we'd have to see it clean. I felt good about our decision to pay the money. Even though our landlord was a first-class stinker, he was an old man, not rich, hard working, and let's face it, what you owe, you owe.

"A very good morning to you, gentlemen. A beautiful morning."

"Hi, Mr. Plotnick," I managed. "How are you feeling?"

"Very well," the landlord beamed, rubbing his hands together with glee. "I had a visit last night from the shoemaker's elves. Magic elves, very generous, and maybe with a little bit of guilt on the conscience."

"He knows!" whispered Don in horror.

"He can't!" I hissed. "If he did, he'd be killing us now!"

Plotnick brought three coffees to our booth. "Very good boys, these elves. One of them, a klutz, fell on the stairs. I was worried for him."

"That was me!" gasped Don as Plotnick walked away. "He *does so* know!"

"Then why is he smiling?" whispered Ferguson.

As if on cue, a tall man in a business suit rushed into the deli, leaving his car running outside.

"Great news, Mr. Plotnick. The insurance company is paying in full." He handed over an envelope. "And here's your check — three hundred and thirty dollars." And he rushed out and drove away.

In our booth, we turned to stone. Now we knew why Plotnick was at peace with the world. Between our consciences and his insurance, he'd been paid for the window *twice*!

"No wonder you're in such a good mood," I managed to choke out.

"That has nothing to do with it," said the landlord self-righteously. "I'm always happy when the first of the month is coming."

"The first of the month? When?"

"Ah, you've forgotten, Mr. Cardone. Tuesday, that's when."

We got up and ran straight upstairs to count our financial resources. I did the stairs in record time, and pounced on our checkbook. Figures don't lie, no matter how you try to juggle them. We didn't have enough money for the August rent.

Hoping for a mistake, I counted our assets. For a lousy planner, I was a great accountant. We had $75 in cash, and $200 or so in the bank, and we were facing a $685 rent check.

I got so freaked out that my eyes unfocused, and the room was a blur. I just said, "Oh."

Then there was Don. "What are we going to do? What are we going to do? What are we going to do? There's no *payday* between now and Tuesday!"

Even Ferguson was unnerved. "We're in big trouble."

"It's all your fault, Peachfuzz!" Don accused. "You and your stupid mistake!"

"The real mistake wasn't the hubcap," said Ferguson tersely. "It was the money."

"Or you, Jason!" Don exploded. "What's that dumb checkbook for — doodles? Why didn't you warn us we didn't have enough money for the rent?"

"I made a mistake!" I babbled.

"Another mistake! I'm surrounded by mistakes! What are we going to do?"

"We could always ask our parents to front us the money," suggested Ferguson.

"No way," I said. "My folks would look at it as an excuse to drag me home."

"Mine, too," said Don. "No more stupid ideas, Peachfuzz! You're the big executive! Why aren't you rich?"

"Because I didn't let Plotnick be my manager!" Ferguson snapped.

"Rootbeer!" I exclaimed. "He's our only hope!"

"He has less than we do," said Don, "even with the toilet brush."

"He's got the harp," I argued. "He can hock it."

We looked over at Rootbeer's corner. There sat his paper bag of underwear, with the knitting needles, stamp albums, Parcheesi game, and his other discarded hobbies. The harp was gone.

"Oh, no!" moaned Don. "Could it have been stolen?"

"Are you crazy?" returned Ferguson. "Only King Kong could steal that harp!"

"He's hocking it!" I exclaimed. "We're saved!"

"Not necessarily," said the Peach. "What if he got another hobby?"

We fought about it all afternoon, and no matter

146

how we sliced it, it all came up Rootbeer. Not that we were so thrilled about asking the universal dispenser of Bad Luck to hand over his hard-earned cash. The entire summer, which I now knew was not the sunshine and roses that the boy from Owen Sound thought it would be, had come down to $685 we didn't have.

There were problems. One — what if Rootbeer said no? Two — what if Rootbeer got mad? Three — where *was* Rootbeer? With a flaky guy like him, "See ya later," could mean a twenty-minute absence or a trip around the world.

Being behind the financial eight ball, we had two dates with Jessica to cancel. Don blew off his afternoon rendezvous with a phony sore throat. Ten minutes later, Ferguson called to weasel out of the evening slot, and confessed the whole thing, to Don's dismay. Jessica offered her life savings, thirty-eight bucks, but manfully, they turned her down. I would have taken it, but she never offered it to me.

"I can't believe you, Peachfuzz!" roared Don. "Why'd you have to make it look like I told her a lie?"

"Because you did."

"And you should have backed me up. You should have said you caught my sore throat!"

"A sore throat isn't very creative," Ferguson decided. "People expect more of me. Maybe — pellagra, elephantiasis, scurvy — "

"So next time *you* pick the disease!"

Then — perfect timing — my mother called.

"Hi, dear. How's everything?"

"Great." Terrible.

"What's new?"

"Nothing." Bankruptcy. Eviction. Death.

In the background, Ferguson and Don were starting to fight again.

"Jason, what's that noise? It sounds like an argument!"

"Uh — no, Mom. We're watching a war movie on TV."

"How are Ferguson and Don?"

"Fine," I said, stepping in between them. "They both send their regards."

"Hi, Mrs. Cardone," they called into the receiver, and resumed their bickering.

"So, are you going someplace fun today?"

"Oh, sure." The street, with all Joe's furniture.

"That's lovely, dear. Your father wants to say hello."

My dad came on. "Hi, son. Flat broke yet, ha-ha?"

"No way, Dad." At least, not till Tuesday.

"I ran into Doug Champion at the bowling alley last night, and we talked about how proud we are of you kids. We had our doubts, but you're sure showing us. Keep it up, son. So long."

" 'Bye, Dad."

Grimly we settled in to wait for Rootbeer.

He came at four in the morning, and was greeted by three very light sleepers. My hopes were dashed almost immediately. He was carrying the Betelgeuse T-5000 Deluxe High Magnification Telescope. It looked expensive. It looked like the August rent.

I was too frazzled for tact. "You have to return it!"

"I could do that," said Rootbeer thoughtfully, "but they might not like it too much back at the store. It's a little broken."

"How broken?" asked Don fearfully.

"The telescope's okay," Rootbeer assured us, "but all the glass fell out."

"It's defective!" I cried. "They *have* to take it back!"

Rootbeer looked vaguely ashamed. "Well, it kind of happened when I hit that guy." He then occupied himself with stacking his harp music on top of the stamp albums.

"Now what?" whispered Ferguson desperately.

"He's still our only hope," I hissed. "None of the rest of us can come up with fast money."

"Oh, God," said Ferguson. "You're asking the guy to go out and get clobbered by a two-by-four."

I shrugged lamely. "Maybe he'll just bite tires or something. Look, I wouldn't ask him if there was any other way! Joe's lease is on the line here!" I cleared my throat very carefully. "Uh — Rootbeer, you wouldn't happen to have any money left, would you?"

"Sure." He shook the upper-right-hand corner of his poncho, and a shower of coins hit the floor, along with a few elastics and paper clips. He looked down for a quick count. "On second thought, I'm broke. How about that."

"Oh, wow, Rootbeer," I moaned. "We've got kind of an emergency. Our rent is due on Wednesday, and we're short more than $400."

Rootbeer whistled, the longer beard hairs rustling in the breeze. "That's a few bucks. Lucky for us it's carnival season. Just let me grab some Z's." And he flopped right down on the floor and was asleep at once.

Summerfest was a giant carnival in the north end of the city. Three bumpkins from Owen Sound were very impressed. There were rides, activity booths, exhibits, and carnival games. Junk food was everywhere. All three of us went along, mostly out of curiosity. What would Rootbeer find to do at a fair like this that would bring us our rent money? Ninety percent of the crowd was under the age of eight.

Ten feet inside the front gate, our savior handed over fifty precious cents at the Test Your Strength booth. He swung the hammer and hit that thing so hard that not only did he ring the bell, he broke the machine for good and always. This won him dirty looks and a kewpie doll worth substantially less than fifty cents.

"Isn't it great?" said Rootbeer, pleased.

"Maybe," I admitted grudgingly. "But, Rootbeer, we have to pay the rent. Plotnick doesn't accept kewpie dolls on account."

"On account of he prefers money," Ferguson finished.

Rootbeer was unconcerned. "Hey, look — Skeeball!"

Rootbeer had a lot of fun that day, and won a lot of prizes, none of which would have counted for two cents at the Olympiad Delicatessen. Also, he was spending money, and making none. We were getting desperate, and kind of tired from carrying an assortment of stuffed toys, pennants, posters, balloons, T-shirts, buttons, and a giant plush water buffalo that was just under actual size. I kept hinting that it must be pretty near time to go for the money. But then Rootbeer would say, "Hey, look — " and we'd have to tour the haunted house, or throw a baseball at some milk bottles, or get on another stomach-turning ride.

On the Enormo-Coaster, Don lost his grip on the stuffed water buffalo. It sailed through the air and landed right in the dolphin pool, where it sank like a rock. The dolphins scattered. I don't blame them. And by the time we got off the ride, the giant toy had soaked up so much water that it had to be lifted out of the pool by crane. We walked by and pretended we'd never seen it before in our lives.

By this time, I'd given up on the idea of paying the rent. But Rootbeer pointed to the Arena, where a sign declared MEET LIVE WRESTLING STARS. We followed him, carrying the spoils, minus the water buffalo.

Inside was a madhouse. A three-thousand-seat hockey arena was packed to the rafters, and all attention was focused on a small ring, where six of the most famous faces in wrestling were putting on exhibitions.

When we walked in, Megaman the Towering Dynamo had a sleeper hold on some poor contestant from the audience. He slammed the guy effortlessly to the ground, and pinned his shoulders. The referee counted three, and the audience went wild.

"That was Ralph from Mississauga. Better luck next

time," said the ring announcer, his voice echoing throughout the building. *"Who'll be our next contestant? For five dollars, you can fight one of our wrestling superstars. If you stay in the ring for sixty seconds, we'll give you one hundred dollars cash!"*

Oh, my God! My heart skipped a beat. Surely this wasn't how Rootbeer planned to make money! A two-by-four was a two-by-four, but these were live professional killers!

"Come on," coaxed the announcer. *"Who will come forward and face Mako Wako the Shark Man?"*

"Hey," said Don suddenly. "Where's Rootbeer?"

Ferguson saw him first, and pointed. "There — getting into the ring."

The three of us ran screaming towards ringside, kewpie dolls flying in all directions.

"And our next contestant is Rootbeer from Toronto, facing Mako Wako the Shark Man. Good luck, Rootbeer." The crowd booed lustily.

"No-o-o-o-o!" howled Don.

I stared in horror. Rootbeer was bigger than Mako, but not by much, and the professional's muscles looked harder than iron. On his fierce head he wore the upper jaw of a shark, and his body, which would have made Joe Cardone look like a ninety-eight-pound weakling, was covered in shark fins.

"We can't let him do this for *us!*" I quavered. "This monster makes his living fighting guys!"

The Peach was looking critically up at the ring. "Maybe Rootbeer can take him."

The bell rang and Mako, three hundred pounds of fierce fighting machine, dealt Rootbeer a mighty smash to the chest. Rootbeer was unmoved, but the Hope Diamond tumbled from the poncho, rolled across the ring, dropped off the apron, and shattered on the floor.

Rootbeer looked annoyed. "Hey! Lay off my stuff!"

Mako readied another smash, but Rootbeer grabbed him by the fins and lifted him a foot off the floor. Enraged, Mako rained a volley of blows on Rootbeer's face.

I wanted to die. Right before my eyes, our loyal friend was getting his face punched in because *I* had forgotten about rent day. All around me, the crowd was cheering encouragement, except for Don, who was hiding his eyes and moaning. The Peach looked on with eager interest.

Suddenly Rootbeer reared back his shaggy head, and brought it forward with the force of a battering ram. Any castle gate would have opened instantly. I'm amazed the Shark Man's head didn't. The conk made *three* echoes. It was like Don's Moontrix coco-bump, times a hundred million.

Mako Wako the Shark Man went limp in Rootbeer's arms. Our hero carried the vanquished wrestler over to his seconds, and set him down quietly outside the ring. Rootbeer was presented with a crisp hundred-dollar bill, which he crumpled up and jammed under the poncho. The three of us cheered ourselves hoarse, but otherwise the crowd was silent.

"Guess what everybody? Rootbeer from Toronto is going to try again." An uneasy murmur passed through the crowd. *"Bring on Brother Barnabas the Holy Terror."*

Brother Barnabas didn't do much better. At the sound of the bell, Rootbeer hurled him bodily out of the ring. Dazed and disoriented, the Holy Terror spent the rest of the sixty seconds trying to climb back in again. And another hundred dollars went under the poncho.

That brought up Captain Concussion the Human Bomb. If the two wrestlers before him had taken Rootbeer a little lightly, the Captain would not make the same mistake. He was ready to give this amateur a taste of real, all-out competition. At the bell, he threw a running body slam at the upstart challenger. I already knew that the Captain was history. This stuff was Rootbeer's specialty. What could a human bomb do that a two-by-four couldn't? Captain Concussion bounced off like a Ping-Pong ball, and hit the canvas flat on his back. Before he could regroup, Rootbeer sat on him, and the poor man was forced to endure what must have been the longest sixty seconds of his career. He floundered like a fish out of water, but was unable to get up.

By this time, the three thousand fans were heading for the exits, and the Arena rang with boos and catcalls. I guess people didn't like to see their TV heroes mashed to a pulp. I was insulted on Rootbeer's behalf. Didn't these fans realize they were watching the greatest natural fighter in the world?

But the show must go on, and that was bad news for Billy Baxter the Bull Moose, Megaman the Towering Dynamo, and Plow Horse the Farm Executioner. Rootbeer was just hitting his stride, and one by one, down they went. He didn't have to go sixty seconds with any of them, because not one lasted ten seconds with him. Plow Horse, the last, wound up in the seventh row of seats, which was empty by that time.

"Come back, folks!" the announcer was pleading. *"There's lots of action still to come! Honest! Let's have some more challengers! And let's have a big hand for Rootbeer, who is LEAVING RIGHT NOW! Come on, people! The action's just begun! Step right up . . . aw, nuts!"*

We ate and celebrated, and tried to let our roommate know how proud we were of him. He seemed surprised that we should think anything unusual had happened.

"We needed money, so we got some," he said.

It was his only comment on his wrestling performance, because he was concentrating fully on the biggest snack I've ever seen. I never thought it was possible to inhale hot dogs, but Rootbeer was full of surprises that day.

We stayed another hour, enjoying the fair, but it was too crowded now that the Arena was empty. So when Rootbeer had had his fill of games and rides, we headed for the parking lot.

We left through the main gate and stopped short. There they were, waiting for us — Mako Wako the Shark Man, Brother Barnabas the Holy Terror, Captain Concussion the Human Bomb, Billy Baxter the Bull Moose, Megaman the Towering Dynamo, and Plow Horse the Farm Executioner — six angry, humiliated wrestlers. We gathered our three sets of puny muscles around Rootbeer.

"Go away!" I barked at the line of brawn. "Rootbeer beat you fair and square!"

Brother Barnabas shook his great big tonsured head. "We weren't ready."

"You don't want to do this," said Rootbeer quietly.

"You deliberately went in there to make us look bad!" snarled Plow Horse.

"I bet you're a pro," added Mako, "making monkeys of the competition!"

The line advanced menacingly, blocking out the sun.

In movies sometimes, the hero jumps off the burning boat a split second before the explosion, and gets to float in triumph for a couple of minutes before he sees the first piranha. It's a lot like life. There we were, down and out, and then we beat the odds — we had the rent money. And suddenly we were all going to die in a North Toronto parking lot. These six monsters were furious with Rootbeer for wrecking their show. We couldn't let Rootbeer fight alone, even though I was pretty sure we'd be zero help. Ferguson and Don must have been thinking the same thing, because all three of us stepped in front of our friend.

"Those poor guys," said Rootbeer, shaking his head sadly. We thought he was talking about *us*. But he pushed us out of the way, and I mean *pushed*. The three of us went flying, stumbling into parked cars. I smacked my head against the mirror of a pickup truck, and by the time I regained my senses and looked back to see if Rootbeer was still alive, it was all over. The six pros lay scattered like tenpins, and Rootbeer was scanning the parking lot for the Camaro.

"What happened?"

"It was like the end of the world," said Ferguson with awed reverence, "and you missed it!"

Rootbeer had a simpler explanation. "Those guys," he said, "they had *bad luck.*"

I handed in the rent money right on time first thing Wednesday morning.

"Ah, Mr. Cardone, you made it," approved Plotnick. "I was really absorbed in the drama. What did Mr. Racinette have to do — eat a house?"

I smiled. "That's kid stuff."

AUGUST

Ten

When I went down to the deli Thursday morning to see if I could borrow an egg for my daily fix of cake mix, I found Plotnick bent over like a boomerang by his griddle.

" 'Neither a borrower nor a lender be,' Mr. Cardone. Fifty cents."

I picked a letter from Joe out of the pile of mail on the counter. "Are you okay, Mr. Plotnick?" The bruise on his head was almost gone, but why was he leaning like that?

"I'll be okay when you give me my fifty cents. Otherwise, no egg."

"But what's with the — ?" I assumed his crouched position.

He scowled from down there. "You want to know what it is? I'll tell you what it is. Mind your own business, that's what it is."

But I could tell he was in pain, because he was grim and pale, and he was abusing his customers even more than usual. And as the day progressed, every time I passed by the deli our landlord looked a little stiffer and a little more bent over. Finally, at dinnertime, when I brought Don and Ferguson to observe the situation, Plotnick had locked up into a miter joint. His tenants were crowded around him, all sympathy and advice.

"What is this — a side show? You're going to order, or what?"

"Mr. Plotnick," reasoned Ferguson, "you're in no condition to be working."

"Congratulations, Mr. Peach. You graduated medical school since this morning. Shut up."

But after a long argument, we managed to hustle our landlord out of the deli and into the Camaro for a ride to the hospital. Getting him into the plush bucket seat was a major operation. Bent up like a coat hanger, he perched there, his head pressing against the glove compartment.

"I wouldn't buy a car like this for no money," he said, obviously overcome with gratitude at our concern.

Plotnick had refused to go and leave the deli unattended, so this was a compromise. Ferguson and Don would drive him to Emergency, and I would stay and mind the store for an hour or so. I only made one sandwich, but I managed to serve coffee, and soup, hand out bills, and work the cash register. It was definitely easier than trying to keep apartment 2C and its inhabitants in shape. I kind of enjoyed it.

The Camaro came back at quarter past eight, and by then, the deli was empty. They got out of the car, first Ferguson, and then Don. The picture looked so normal that it took a second for the question to bubble up.

"Where's Plotnick?"

"He's not coming back," Ferguson announced emotionally.

"*What?!*"

"Peachfuzz, you jerk!" Don exploded. "What did you tell you him like that for? Yes, he's coming back eventually, but not tonight. And guess whose fault it is? *Peachfuzz's!*"

"But that doctor said he was okay!" I protested.

"His head is fine," Ferguson explained, "but he racked up his back. They put him in traction."

"But how?" I wailed. "He was perfect just yesterday!"

"It took a while to stiffen up," said Don unhappily. "But now that it has, he's in for a month."

"A month?" My heart gave a lurch. "And it's — it's *our fault*!" I slumped against the counter. Talk about revenge going sour! We were supposed to be grown men, out in the world. How could we have let a kiddie prank get so out of hand? Boy, we were big city guys, all right. We were practically a street gang. And now a defenseless old man was in the hospital because of us.

My mourning was interrupted by the ringing of the deli phone. It was Plotnick.

"Mr. Cardone, this is your fault! You come and break me out of here! They've got me tied up like a common criminal, and the doctors won't listen to reason. It's like Russia!"

I tried to be soothing. "You'll be all right, Mr. Plotnick. You're not tied up; you're in traction. It's for your back."

"What good is health when the world is coming to an end? I'm not a rich man, Mr. Cardone! My tenants pay tiny little rents, and my restaurant barely makes a living as it is!"

The guilt was eating me up. "Mr. Plotnick — " I said. I never think when I'm emotionally upset. All I knew was that we owed this man a hell of a lot more than a box of candy and a get-well card. "Don't worry about the deli. *I'll* run it."

Ferguson and Don stared at me.

"You? Hah!" came the response over the phone. "You wouldn't know a cheese blintz from the U.S.S. *Constitution*!"

That did it. "I'll have you know I've been doing a lot of cooking lately."

"I'll be out of business in a week!"

"No, you won't," I snapped with grim determination. "When you get back, you won't know the place, it'll be running so great."

I waited for a thank you. Plotnick just said, "Oi!" and hung up.

Ferguson whistled. "Boy, Jason, you're in for it now. This is a fourteen-hour-a-day job, no weekends off."

I picked up Plotnick's meat fork and shook it at him. "Mind your own business, Mr. Peach."

We laughed. I was getting the hang of it already.

* * *

164

Because I didn't have a potbelly like the previous proprietor, Plotnick's apron billowed around me like a bivouac tent. Fifteen minutes after opening, an end had found its way into the grill, and was on fire. Wayne Gretzky's Sister helped me put myself out, and I returned to my eggs, waffles, and pancakes.

It took some doing. Some people had to wait a little longer than usual, but I made it through breakfast just fine. I told everybody that Plotnick was on vacation in the Caribbean, and God's Grandmother promised to spread the word around the building to back me up. I'm not usually a liar, but my conscience just couldn't handle the real explanation.

It would have been better if Plotnick hadn't called (long distance from the Caribbean) five times to talk me through the morning.

"So, are you having a good time, Mr. Plotnick? How's the weather?"

"You're maybe crazy, Mr. Cardone? I'm hanging up here like a barbecued chicken, and you're talking about the weather?"

"Great. Have you been to the beach?"

"No, I haven't been to the beach! Now listen — when that gangster from the meat company delivers, weigh everything on *our* scale, not his. And when the baker comes, count all the hot dog buns. He's a criminal."

Things quieted down until lunch, when a flurry of takeout orders came for deli sandwiches. I just sliced and slapped and wrapped while talking to Plotnick on the phone, which was wedged up against my ear. If my neck and shoulder stayed like that much longer, the hospital was going to have to save a little traction for me.

"Don't overfill, Mr. Cardone! I can hear you're overfilling!"

"No kidding! You went snorkeling? What a vacation! Don't disturb yourself by calling again."

The takeout orders tapered off around two, so I had plenty of time to clean up the place and get ready for the dinner hour. The first customers began trickling in around four-thirty, and among them was none other than Rootbeer Racinette.

He didn't look up. He just mumbled, "Coffee, Plotnick," and crammed himself into our booth.

I served him with a flourish, put on my best Plotnick voice, and said, "So, Mr. Racinette, you're going to eat or what?"

"Hi, Jason, what are you doing here?"

"Covering for Plotnick for a few days," I said. "Hey, you don't look so hot. Something wrong?"

"I think I'm getting executive burnout," said Rootbeer seriously. "That telescope just isn't doing it for me. I see just as good without it."

I suppressed a smile, thinking of the shattered lenses. Rootbeer was looking through an empty tube.

"Last night really got me down," Rootbeer continued sadly. "I discovered this whole new constellation. I mean, it wasn't on any of my star charts. I phoned the Astronomical Society hot line, and right while I was talking, my constellation lit up." He looked embarrassed. "It said 'Goodyear.' That really stressed me out."

So he ordered three giant dinners, and ate them all.

"Any dessert?" I inquired, clearing the plates away. It was a joke, but Rootbeer nodded vigorously.

"Better let me have some of that Cardone Surprise."

"We don't serve that here," I told him.

The giant's face fell. "Really? I was kind of psyched for it."

I scanned the deli. There was just Rootbeer, Romeo and Juliet, and a few others who were in the middle of their meals and wouldn't need attention for a while.

"Watch the cash register." I ran upstairs, grabbed our box of D-Lishus chocolate fudge cake mix, and smuggled it into the deli kitchen. I mixed up a quick batch, stealing frequent tastes for myself, and stuck some in one of Plotnick's tall glass ice cream dishes. We didn't have any strawberries, so I threw in chopped nuts and candy sprinkles, and topped the whipped cream off with a cherry. I was amazed. It looked like a real dessert.

Rootbeer went into ecstasy, and the Cardone Surprise was gone in three seconds.

"Hey," called Romeo. "Let me have what he's having."

So I made one for him, too, two spoons.

"It's fantastic!" Juliet approved. "What is it?"

"Trade secret," I said smugly.

"I've definitely had this before," said Romeo.

I smiled. Who hadn't licked the spoon while Mom baked a cake?

"I know this flavor. I just can't place it." He motioned to a man sitting at the counter. "Hey, Ernie, you've got to try some of this."

I sold three more Cardone Surprises, but then we were all out. And I got a great tip from everybody who tried one. For the first time since my previous life as a feeder at Plastics Unlimited, I had cash that I'd earned with my own two hands. And I hadn't had to pick up the Employment section, or make a single call. Not bad.

Don got fired from the publishing company; the charge — laziness. But instead of throwing himself into the want ads, he tucked a towel into his waistband and came down to the deli with me.

"Doesn't this bring back the good old days of Plastics Unlimited?" he said nostalgically. "You and me, working together, Peachfuzz nowhere in sight — "

"Ever been a waiter before?" I interrupted.

Don shrugged airily. "How hard can it be?"

"This is Plotnick's business we're running, and we're here because we put him in the hospital. We owe him our best."

Don dropped five omelets during breakfast alone. The last, which landed on the Ugly Man's shirt, came while I was on a transcontinental phone call from Plotnick in Aruba.

"What was that noise? I know that noise! No! Don't tell me! It was a breaking dishes noise!"

"Jet-skiing? Wow!"

"When they untie me, Mr. Cardone, you better watch out for yourself!"

As lunch approached, I left Don in charge and

ran to the supermarket to buy ten boxes of D-Lishus chocolate fudge cake mix. When I returned, Mr. Wonderful was comfortably established in a booth with a brunette while my customers waited.

"Hey, can we get some service over here?"

"In a minute," called Don impatiently. His eyes never left the object of his attentions.

I ran over to the irate man. "Is there a problem, sir?"

"Darn right! That ninny over there won't take my order!"

So *I* took his order, and *I* cooked, and served, and fielded calls from Plotnick while Don shmoozed.

Finally I could bear it no longer. It was the height of the lunch hour, the deli was full, and there were Don and that girl, taking up a whole table for one fifty-cent cup of coffee. So I grabbed Mr. Wonderful by the shoulders and dragged him back to work. While we were arguing, his girl ran out on the check.

Don was livid. "I had her in the palm of my hand, Jason! You owe me one girl!"

"This isn't a game!" I hissed. "Clear some of those tables."

So he did, but his heart wasn't in it. And it wasn't long before I overheard him on the phone, fighting with Kiki's mother this time over whether or not Kiki did, in fact, exist and, if so, at what number.

Between keeping Don in line and running the place single-handedly, I didn't get a chance to whip up any Cardone Surprise until dinner. I made a giant batch in Plotnick's blender, and added a little card to all the menus advertising that, for only $1.95 more, my patrons could experience the miracle of Cardone Surprise.

Not one person ordered it. I flogged the dessert section to death with every table I waited, but there were no takers. What I really needed was Rootbeer to inhale an order with his usual oohing and aahing and smacking of lips. So I went up to this one lady, who must have weighed two hundred and fifty pounds, and knew a good dessert when she tasted one, because she'd obviously tried them all, and said, "All of our *entreés* include a complimentary dessert *du jour*." I placed a beautifully decorated Cardone Surprise in front of her, and stepped back, holding my breath.

Boy, had I ever picked the right lady. Much better than Rootbeer, who was on the outside of his food in one or two gulps, she savored every drop, raving loudly, and begging for the recipe. She hadn't even finished before I started on my second blenderful, because the whole first batch was sold and gone.

"I've had this before," she announced, ordering another. "It's so familiar. It's a memory — a chocolate memory."

So out came the menu cards advertising Cardone Surprise, and in went new ones pushing the Chocolate Memory.

I sold nineteen Chocolate Memories with a very little bit of help from Don, who was too busy chatting up the young female customers. As the dinner crowd was tapering off around eight-thirty, I was on the phone with Plotnick when suddenly our landlord interrupted me, shouting, "What was that? What was that?"

"What?" I looked up. In the corner booth, Don was waiting on a couple with a baby who had just barfed all over the table. I shuddered. The kid was a bottomless pit! I didn't think there was that much barf in the whole world, let alone inside one little baby.

I admit it was disgusting, but Don wasn't taking it very professionally. He was standing there with his hand over his mouth, looking like he was doing his level best not to add to the baby's contribution. I tossed him a towel, and he stared at me like I was crazy.

"Clean it up," I said.

"Why me?"

"Why not you? I've got Plotnick on the phone, the soup is boiling over, and you're right there."

Don approached me, his voice confidential. "Listen, Jason, I've got a list in my mind of all the things I'm never going to do in this life, and that's on it. Pretty high up, too." He threw the towel back to me.

What could I do? I fired him.

"Good for you, Mr. Cardone!" approved Plotnick from the Caribbean. "He's got no respect for the customers."

"Ha!" I snorted. "*You* would have charged the baby for a new restaurant!"

"Just a tablecloth."

My routine was becoming settled. At six A.M. I'd rush down to the deli, put on the coffee, and begin heating up the grill. The Stripper was usually just coming home from work, so I'd mix her a double Alka-Seltzer cocktail and send her upstairs. Then I'd lock up and go out for my morning run. By the time I came back and showered, I was ready to open for the day.

When I descended on Friday morning, I found Jessica sitting on the doorstep, clipboard in hand. I didn't figure she wanted breakfast.

"I'm very busy," I said evenly.

She followed me inside and poured two coffees for us. "It's my final project," she explained, "and it's due today. We have to plan a whole week of nutritionally balanced menus for a family of four."

I pointed to the top paper, which was blank. "I guess they're on a crash diet, eh?"

She laughed and laughed, and told me what a great sense of humor I had.

"It wasn't a joke," I growled, writing up a bill for her coffee. "Since you're the one taking the course, and you haven't written anything down, then I guess that poor family's going to starve, aren't they?"

"Well," she said sheepishly, "I was kind of hoping you'd help me."

I shook my head. "You can't pull the wool over my eyes. You're not looking for help. You want me to do it for you."

She beamed. "Jason, you're a lifesaver! And I promise — it'll only take two seconds."

Well, at least it was the final project. After this she'd be Ferguson's and Don's problem exclusively.

No sooner did I open up her nutrition textbook

than she began to lose interest. Soon I was totaling up saturated fats while she read the paper. A few minutes later, the radio was blaring in my ear.

"Do you mind?" I snarled. "I'm doing *your* work! The least you can do is give me a little peace and quiet!"

"Sorry. Here, I'll help. I really will." But a few minutes later, she was wandering around again, reading the choking instructions and the fire laws.

Then the breakfast customers started to arrive. While I poured, cooked, served, and cleared away, she replaced me over the clipboard. She didn't write one word.

"Is that your girlfriend?" God's Grandmother asked coyly.

"No, she's everybody else's girlfriend. She only drops by every now and then to let me do her homework."

After the breakfast rush, we got back to work, except her. She was pacing around in the show window, peering outside and scowling.

"Look at all that garbage. Apple cores, newspapers, pop cans — no wonder the streets aren't safe."

The leap of logic escaped me. "Garbage is dangerous?"

"It's a statistically proven fact that the crime rate is lower in cities with less litter. What does that say to you?"

I looked up from her homework. "Criminals are slobs?"

"No, no, no," she said impatiently. "I belong to a group called 'Clean Streets Are Safe Streets.' Four times a year we all get together for a major city cleanup, and the cops confirm that street crime goes down in the areas that are really clean. Too bad you're stuck in the deli. Our next sweep is tomorrow." I thanked God for the deli. She sat down at a booth and sighed. "I'm kind of disappointed in Ferguson and Don, though. Neither of them was interested in volunteering. There's no room in my life for people without social responsibility."

How about schoolwork responsibility? Not picking up garbage was a crime against humanity, but goofing off while a guy, not even your boyfriend, slaved over your assignments — that was okay?

And when she ran off to class with my finished project — late, of course — I noticed that she'd forgotten to pay for the coffee.

"Hey, Jason, guess what? Jessica pulled an A in home ec."

This was the news that greeted me when I got up to the apartment that night after closing time. The Peach always did have great timing.

I Frisbeed the snapshot of Joe and Melina on the beach at Mykonos right at his face. "She must have worked like a Trojan!" I said acidly.

"Hey, I thought it was pretty good news," said Don, mystified. "I never knew she could cook."

"Yeah," I replied. "She hid that from me, too."

I was surprised that the two of them could discuss Jessica without a fight breaking out. But later that evening, Don pulled me aside confidentially. "Don't say anything about this to Peachfuzz," he murmured. "Jessica belongs to this group of weirdos who go around picking up garbage 'cause you can't get mugged if the street's too clean. She doesn't know it, but I'm going down there tomorrow to surprise her. She thinks I'm not interested. Man, is she A-one right! But when she sees me out there slinging crap, I'll have Peachfuzz massacred!''

Half an hour later, the Peach sauntered over. ''I know I promised to help you in the deli tomorrow, Jason, and I will. But I need to take off a couple of hours in the morning. Jessica's on this cleanup crew for a really worthy cause, and I want to go down and help out. Just don't say anything to Don.''

I had trouble getting to sleep that night, even though I was really bushed. If I had it figured right, Don and Ferguson were both going to roar downtown to impress Jessica, and meet head-on. The biggest mess that cleanup crew would face could very easily be the chunks of human flesh my two best friends were going to tear out of each other.

Eleven

The next morning, I pretended to be asleep, but I had one eye on Don Champion. He rose furtively from his bed on the couch, hopped athletically over Rootbeer's sleeping hulk, and tiptoed to the bathroom.

"Occupied," came the Peach's voice.

"What? Hurry up!"

Splashing, spitting, banging on door. Then they switched, and soon it was Ferguson clamoring to get in.

"Go away! You've had your chance!"

"Shhh. You'll wake up the whole building."

They dressed at the same time, silently, looking

daggers at one another. At last, Ferguson broke the ice.

"Where are you off to?" he asked casually.

"Wouldn't you like to know?" Pause, less certainly, "Where are *you* going?"

But the Peach had clammed up again. And when Don stepped into the bathroom to sculpt his hair, Ferguson sprinted out of the apartment.

I waited for Don to come out of the bathroom, but all I got was dead silence. Not even Mr. Wonderful brushed his hair for this long. So I got up and looked. The bathroom was empty, but the window was open, the air conditioner askew.

I knew then and there that the Olympiad Delicatessen was going to be closed this morning. Jason Cardone, proprietor, was needed elsewhere to prevent a bloodbath.

"We have a severe thunderstorm warning in effect for Toronto and all surrounding regions. The humidity is one hundred percent, the pollution is over the danger level, and the Department of Health advises joggers to pass up today and stay in the air conditioning."

Thus spake the radio as I tooled the Camaro along Bloor Street, looking for the cleanup crew. I found them at the corner of Yonge Street, the busiest and dirtiest intersection in town, about thirty or forty young people with pointed sticks and heavy-duty garbage bags. I scanned for Jessica. Where she was, could Don and the Peach be far behind?

Then I saw them — two furious gladiators, squaring off, pointed sticks aimed at each other's pancreases. Jessica was running in circles around them, trying to make peace. I have no idea why she didn't just neutralize each one with a shot from her brass knuckles keychain. I mean, we'd already proved that it worked.

With a squeal of tires, I pulled into the nearest parking space, and leaped out. I hit the road running.

"Stop! *Stop!*"

Suddenly both pointed sticks were aimed at *my* pancreas. "You told!" they chorused.

Then, hearing each other, they resumed their standoff. I had a brief giddy vision of myself trying to explain to Mrs. Peach and Mrs. Champion that these two shish kebabs used to be their sons.

Jessica saved the day. "Put those weapons down or I'll never speak to either of you again as long as I live!" The sticks dropped to the road. "Now, either clean up, or go home!" She sent Mr. Wonderful and the Peach to opposite sides of the street, and before I knew it, I was being issued a litterbag, too.

"Oh, no," I said seriously. "I was just — uh — spectating."

"Come on, Jason," she wheedled. "You don't have to stay all day. Just help us out for an hour or so."

I was wary. I already knew what it was like to be recruited by Jessica for "two seconds." "An hour or so" could take weeks!

"Please — "

I decided to stay, just to keep an eye on my volatile friends. Jessica cheered, and told me I was wonderful, and threw her arms around me, and kissed me on the cheek. I glared at her.

178

In a gutter choked with yesterday's newspapers, soaked in engine oil, I set to work, stabbing and stuffing. Thunder rumbled.

The wind picked up, gusting down the street, and suddenly all the litter was in full flight. A few of us were stabbing at the air. I actually caught myself thinking, *Stop that! You'll put someone's eye out!* Uh-oh. Another of my mother's specialties.

The Saturday morning shopping crowd stood on the sidewalk and gawked, but they weren't watching us — at least, not all of us. Ferguson had put down his stick, and was walking around in circles, holding up his index finger to the wind. Every now and then, he would lick his finger to help him gauge exactly the spot he was looking for. Satisfied at last, he nodded to himself, and stopped right in the middle of the road. There he stood motionless, his bag held open, oblivious to the honking of car horns and the curses of motorists. A murmur spread through the crowd.

Even Don was paying attention. "What's he trying to do?" he asked.

The parting of the Red Sea couldn't have been a better spectator event. Suddenly a big gust of wind came up, lifted half the garbage on the block, and blew it straight into Ferguson's bag. It was amazing. I wouldn't put it ahead of Rootbeer and the wrestlers, but I think it might have edged out the two-by-four.

Yonge Street went wild. The shoppers all broke into applause, and motorists were honking and flashing their lights. A lot of our group mobbed the Peach, and he was an instant hero, to Don's great disgust. Even Jessica sort of forgave him.

179

"Well, I'd better go open the deli," I began, sensing an opportunity to get myself out of there. But at that very second, there was a blinding flash of lightning and a crash of thunder that shook the ground under our feet. The sky opened up and let us have it. Did it rain! No drops, just sheets of water pounding down on us.

The Clean Streets Are Safe Streets crew scattered. Apparently wet streets were empty streets.

Jessica was furious. "Where's everybody going?" she cried. "We can't let a little rain get in our way!"

Ferguson and Don grabbed her, and I led the way to the Camaro. Only it wasn't there.

"Where's the car, Jason?" called Don. "We're getting soaked!"

I stared. Yes, this was definitely my parking space. Now, anybody else would have figured the car had been stolen. But I knew better. Stolen was something I could only dream about. Was there any doubt? A certain Camaro was — why, why, *why*? — still on the hot sheet.

Ferguson read the look on my face. "Not the cops — ?"

"Aw, man!" moaned Don. With no car to give us shelter, his first impulse was to save his clothes. Ruthlessly he overturned his garbage bag and dumped its contents out onto the road — right in front of Jessica, who was horrified. Then he ripped a few quick holes and made himself a raincoat.

Jessica refused to leave because, as she put it, "It's already starting to clear up." So we left her under an awning and swam to the nearest police station.

180

It was horrible, going through the story all over again, especially since I was going to have to say it one more time when we got to the unit that actually had the car, and give a third performance for our neighborhood station, where the original report had been filed. Those were the idiots who had guaranteed that my troubles were over. What was so difficult about canceling one computer entry?

At last, word came through from 54 Division that the Camaro was okay. I was positive I could hear laughing on the other end of the line. Big joke.

"Make sure you take my car off the stolen list!" I yelled at the phone, and there was more laughing.

It was four o'clock in the afternoon by the time I opened the deli.

"Are you crazy, Mr. Cardone? Why don't you just drive a knife through my heart and twist it? I've been calling a whole day!"

"It was so busy I couldn't get to the phone."

"You're a liar!"

Great judge of character, our landlord.

Don got another job, the Peach got another promotion, and Rootbeer got another hobby.

Don was an usher in a movie theater, and spent so much time asleep during the show that he was up all night. This gave him an opportunity to try Kiki at three A.M. Kiki's father (or whoever that was) kind of lost it. He screamed about having the calls traced, swore that Kiki was dead, and hung up so hard that I heard the click all the way from the beanbag chair.

Even though Ferguson was still only making

$350 a week, there was no question that he was Harold Robb's wonder boy. Too bad the Peach still had another year of high school ahead of him, because he had Plastics Unlimited in the palm of his hand. He was in on all the important meetings, traveled frequently on business, and had just been presented with his own key to the executive washroom. The Peach had *arrived*.

Rootbeer's new hedge against executive burnout was rock polishing, which was not as bad as the harp, but ten times worse than stamps. He had bought one of those polishing wheels, and not a toy, either. It was the kind jewelers use to finish diamonds, and it must have cost a fortune. Where had he gotten the money? We had a sneaking suspicion it had something to do with a *Toronto Star* headline that read: *Man Uproots Telephone Pole*. Especially since I spent that night digging splinters out of Rootbeer's hamlike hands. But our hero refused to discuss financial matters, as it could only lead to stress, and we all knew what *that* led to.

My own career as the new Plotnick was keeping me pretty busy. On Monday morning, the man from the paper goods company just stared at me when I handed over the money for our napkin shipment.

"You mean that's it?"

I shrugged. "What else is there?"

"Plotnick usually screams and cries and calls me a criminal, and tries to get out of paying the tax. Then he counts all the napkins and pulls out the ones that are creased. I used to hate stopping here."

The meat man put it more succinctly. "I hope Plotnick never comes back."

The popularity of my Chocolate Memory dessert continued to grow, and I was now going through a dozen boxes of D-Lishus cake mix per day. My regulars ordered it all the time, and I was getting patrons from different parts of the city who had come in just to try my new dessert, the flavor everyone could remember but no one could identify. This inspired me to develop the Chocolate Memory *à la mode*, which meant the same old stuff with a scoop of vanilla ice cream. $2.95.

As the week progressed, a peculiar phenomenon happened at the Olympiad. We continued to get our normal mealtime traffic. But a whole new crowd started to come from about six-thirty till closing, and all they wanted was dessert — more specifically, Chocolate Memory, plain and *à la mode*. They weren't a neighborhood crowd, either. They were from all over, the trendy nightlifers, winding the evening down with coffee and dessert. They came from movies and plays, concerts and clubs, baseball games and discotheques, all converging on Pitt Street to eat my raw cake mix. Suddenly the buzz of conversation included such topics as foreign films, political theory, astrology, and funky fashion — all this in Plotnick's restaurant with the salamis in the window.

I was afraid my fellow tenants might object to the crowds and the noise and the late hours. But they seemed to enjoy the excitement, except for the Ugly Man, who hated everything. They were all Chocolate Memory fans anyway, and I did my best to keep their tables, speed them through lines, and give them quick service.

On Friday and Saturday nights, I didn't get to

close until after one in the morning. When I finally managed to kick out the last jet-setting couple and sent them running off into the night musing, "What *is* that wonderful flavor they use?", I grabbed the mile-long register tape and examined it. My estimate was that I pulled in twice as much money from coffee and dessert than from the three meals combined. I wasn't running Plotnick's business into the ground; I was launching it through the roof!

My main problem was space. The deli could seat fifty-five, including seven stools at the counter, which my up-scale dessert crowd stayed away from. And while the people lined up outside were very good for my ego, they weren't filling the cash register unless they were inside and eating. I needed to bump up my seating capacity. Plotnick had a bunch of old beaten-up tables and chairs stored in the basement and, one night, while Don was out with Jessica, Ferguson helped me haul them up.

"Don't worry about leaving space between them," I advised. "If you can get through them turned sideways, it's enough." I looked around critically. "Better take those stools downstairs. That'll make some room."

Ferguson stared at me. "Are you sure about this, Jason? What if Plotnick doesn't like it?"

I dismissed this. "All Plotnick cares about is money. The more tables, the more money."

Ferguson blinked, almost like a computer whose circuits were engaged. "In that case," was his readout, "those booths have to go. They're too bulky. You could get more than double the number of people in that space."

I laughed. "I'm not that crazy." But from that moment on, the thought of the wasted space tormented me. I almost expected the booth people to order a little bit more, and to leave bigger tips, to compensate for taking up all that room so selfishly. I know it's weird, but I really *thought* that.

Tuesday was my busiest night yet. It seemed that, no matter how many tables and chairs I crammed into the deli, the dessert-hungry evening crowd could fill them. I could no longer buy my cake mix from the supermarket. I had to set up a charge account with the D-Lishus Corporation. The stuff was arriving by the truckload.

At around ten o'clock, with a full house and Plotnick pestering me on the phone, I had to drop everything to deal with Mr. Nevin, a weasel-like man who squeezed up to the counter and flashed me a badge that looked like it was at least from the FBI.

"Nevin. Telephone company."

I was relieved. If he was the fire marshal, I had three times as many people in there as I was supposed to.

His eyes narrowed. "Are you Mr. Plotnick?"

"God forbid!" I blurted out. "My name is Cardone. I'm in charge here while Mr. Plotnick's — away."

"We have a complaint against a line in this building — 555-9679."

I gulped. Joe's number.

"Apparently someone named Ron, or Don, has been harassing another of our customers, calling at all hours, and demanding to speak to a 'Kiki.'

185

Now, we traced the calls, and contacted 555-9679 this afternoon. I spoke to a Mr. — " he consulted a notebook, " — Rootbeer? He was not very co-operative." His penetrating eyes raked my face, which must have been chalk-white. "I see this situation is familiar to you."

"Well," I stammered, "I'm in charge of the restaurant. I don't really have anything to do with the apartments." So I live in one. So what? This could mean trouble for Don. Not to mention that my brother Joe wouldn't be too happy to come home from Europe and find that his telephone had been confiscated.

Mr. Nevin was no dummy. "We insist that this must stop, or we'll have to take appropriate action. I'm sure you'll know whom to speak to."

I mumbled, "I really don't — uh — have no idea — doesn't ring a bell — "

He gave me a look that not only said that *he* knew that *I* knew, but also that he was deeply disappointed in me for it. Then, thank God, he left.

I practically threw the last few customers out the door in my anxiety to get upstairs.

Ferguson, Don, and Jessica sat cross-legged in front of the television, playing Nintendo. Jessica's careful bookkeeping system had broken down, and she had scheduled a date with both. An evening at home in my brother's video playground was the compromise.

As for Rootbeer, he had pawned the rock polisher and pushed about eight tons of shiny stones onto the discard pile in the corner. Now he was sprawled out in the midst of a giant deluxe chemistry set, turning clear liquids colored, and performing experiments from a little blue booklet.

"Don," I said, "I've got to talk to you."

"What?" he said absently, manipulating the joystick. On the screen, two video adventurers were wandering through a labyrinth, vigorously decapitating goblins and demons with lightning swordplay.

"I have to see you privately." For his sake, I couldn't very well talk about Kiki in front of Jessica.

"In a minute." His eyes never left the screen.

"It's important," I insisted.

"Give me a break! I'm finally going to beat Peachfuzz. I'm up three beheadings."

I grabbed him by the arm. "Come on!"

Don threw down the joystick in disgust. "Now look what you made me do! I got stepped on by a dragon! Peachfuzz, this game doesn't count!"

I dragged him bodily into the bathroom, and Jessica took over his place.

Don was in a lousy mood. "How the heck did Peachfuzz get so good at video games?"

"Because he's been programming his own since he was three. Shut up and listen. We just got visited by an inspector from the phone company. You can't call Kiki any more. The guy complained, they traced the calls, and we're in big, big trouble!"

Don put his hand to his mouth in horror. "Oh, no."

"What?"

"I just called, while Jessica was in the bathroom! Maybe ten minutes ago! I told the guy if he didn't let me talk to his daughter, I'd resort to desperate measures!"

I gulped. "They wouldn't know that I hadn't warned you yet! It sounds like you're threatening them!"

Don looked anxious. "What can we do?"

I racked my brain. "Maybe if you phone up right now and admit the whole thing — " My breath caught in my throat as I glanced out the window. Pitt Street was swarming with police cruisers. "Oh, my God!"

Uniformed officers were piling out of five squad cars. We squinted at the streetlit scene. They were all holding rifles! I watched, transfixed, as the SWAT team surrounded the building.

"Wow!" breathed Don. "Can you imagine what Plotnick would do if we told him there were rifles trained on his precious property?"

I stared at him in horror and, seeing my face, it hit him, too. "You don't think this has anything to do with — ?"

"The telephone company!" I shrieked.

"But they don't carry guns!" cried Don.

I was hysterical. "They called the cops on us! We have to talk to them! We have to *explain*!" I began to work frantically to open the window. It was stuck.

"Hey, guys," called Rootbeer from the living room. "Come watch my experiment."

I heaved at the window with all my might. It wouldn't budge. Desperately I hurled myself against the air conditioner in an attempt to push it out onto the fire escape.

"Don! Help me!"

The two of us put our backs to it, throwing ourselves painfully against the metal casing. I felt it give a little.

"Last chance," called Rootbeer. "It's going to be amazing."

"Lie down!" yelled Don.

"Lie down!? What are you — *crazy*?"

"We can kick it out!"

We got down on our backs, legs poised in the air, ready to pound the air conditioner with our feet.

Tired of waiting for us, Rootbeer proceeded with his experiment. "Okay, here goes."

"Together!" I commanded. "One — two — !"

"Oops," came Rootbeer's mildly annoyed voice. " — *three!*"

Boom! Rootbeer's experiment blew up with a deafening roar just as Don and I brought our legs forward. We were so shocked by the explosion that our four feet jerked away from our bodies and dealt the air conditioner a tremendous wallop.

It burst out of the window, skittered across the fire escape, and disappeared under the railing. A split second later, there was the sound of a ten thousand BTU cooling system smashing through the roof of a police cruiser.

And then another sound — sharp — terrifying —

Gunfire!

189

Twelve

Yes, they shot up the building, and no, it wasn't the telephone company.

The Chief of Police himself came to explain it to us and to the rest of the tenants, except God's Grandmother, who slept through the whole thing. It had all begun the last time a computer operator had attempted to take the Camaro off the stolen list. He hit the wrong button so, instead of deleting the entry, he bumped it up to *Vehicles Connected With Dangerous Felons*.

"So it's pretty straightforward," the chief said cheerfully. "When our cruiser did a routine check of your license plate, he got a 'Dangerous Felon' flag. He called for backup. That's standard procedure. And during routine deployment of personnel, there was an explosion, and one of our cars was taken out by an unidentified weapon."

"It was an air conditioner!" I wailed.

"Our guys didn't know that. They were going strictly by the book. Anyway, don't worry, folks. It was our mistake, except for the air conditioner."

"We're really sorry about that," quavered Don. "It was an accident. We were just trying to get the window open so we could explain about the phone calls."

The chief grinned. "Oh, yeah, the phone calls. We don't send the SWAT team to check out crank calls. The phone company uses the Air Force." And he walked away, laughing.

Ours was the only apartment that had sustained any damage. The police offered to set us up at a hotel, but since only our bathroom had been hit, we decided to stay put. Unbelievably, the air conditioner was still in great shape, but we didn't have a window to put it in.

Eventually the other tenants tired of the excitement and went back to bed. We followed them upstairs to find Rootbeer scrapping his chemistry set.

"I'm disappointed," was his only comment.

Sleep would not come, so we lay awake, listening to the Phantom raving into the phone about the night's events. Hearing about bombing the police with an air conditioner was even more ridiculous than actually doing it. If it hadn't been us, I would have recommended that the perpetrators be locked in a rubber room.

We went down again to watch the sun rise over

the rubble. As the first rays glinted off the shards of broken glass that lay in front of 1 Pitt Street, we saw the full extent of the damage. Stray bullets had bitten pieces out of the ancient brick and shattered the brand-new show window of the deli.

Don covered his eyes. "If my mom calls," he moaned, "tell her she's got the wrong number. There's no way I could fake a good mood today."

God's Grandmother went out for her morning jog, but the nearsighted old lady still hadn't noticed that anything was out of place at 1 Pitt Street. She just muttered something about poor streetcleaning as her sneakers crunched over the broken glass.

I stood forlornly in the wreckage of my restaurant. With my meat fork, I absently pried a bullet out of the torpedo salami. It had once proudly hung in the show window, center of interest of the string of prepared meats.

"They shot my salami," I said to no one. The telephone rang, so I put down the carcass and went to answer it.

"So, Mr. Cardone, how's my restaurant?"

"Kind of slow this morning," I managed. A better answer would have been "What restaurant?" but how could I tell this poor, sick, old man that he'd been right all along? He *was* out of business.

"Slow? How slow? Your gorilla friend is chasing away my customers?"

"Don't worry," I said. "Last night it was really hectic." Understatement.

"You're a good boy, Mr. Cardone."

That hurt more than an insult. It was the first

civil word he'd ever said to me, and the first time I hadn't deserved it. I hung up feeling even lower than before.

Don pulled by, turned, and parked the Camaro, carefully avoiding the broken glass. He got out carrying a large bag from a twenty-four-hour drugstore. "Soap, toothbrushes, toothpaste, and toilet paper," he announced. "All the stuff they shot."

I could hear him perfectly. Only air separated the deli and the street. "I thought I told you to push that car over a cliff," I said bitterly.

Don shrugged. "I couldn't find one high enough." He and Ferguson were united for the first time all summer in the effort to cheer me up. I doubted that even the magic of Ferguson Peach, super-genius, could accomplish that.

Don came over and put a hand on my shoulder. "Forget it," he said comfortingly. "At least nobody got hurt. That's pretty amazing."

"I guess," I mumbled. "But we put the guy in the hospital, blew up his building, and now we have to walk out on him because there's nothing else we can do."

"Sure there is," said Don. "We can clean this up no sweat."

I looked at him in disgust. "There are times when being an optimist is just plain stupid. Look at this place! I wouldn't even know where to start!"

Rootbeer entered, carefully opening and closing the door even though there was no glass in it. "Coffee," he ordered, as though this were an ordinary morning, and flopped down in our regular booth. Weakened by the wildly ricocheting bullets, the frame collapsed under his weight, and Rootbeer disappeared below seat level, his huge legs jack-knifing into the air.

"Well," he sighed, "no sense keeping these around." He got up and, with one grunt, wrenched the entire line of booths from their moorings, and heaved the whole mess — twelve benches and six tables — out the gaping window and onto the sidewalk.

I stared. There! It was that easy! Where the booths had been lay bare floor, nice and clean. All it took was a little brute strength. I looked at Rootbeer and almost smiled. A lot of brute strength.

Just then the Peach's voice came from inside Plotnick's apartment behind the deli. "Hey, guys, you'd better come in here."

I couldn't stand the suspense. "Just break it to me. Will his insurance cover it?"

"You have to see it to believe it!"

Don and I joined Ferguson in Plotnick's living room. The Peach was standing by a two-drawer filing cabinet that stood amidst the overstuffed Victorian furniture. The grin on his face was pure unholy delight. He showed us a file folder three inches thick. On the top was scrawled *Insurance*.

"He's covered?" I barely whispered.

Ferguson laughed. "Enough to rebuild ten delis. What do you want to bet he makes a profit?"

That was it for me. The smile hit, my first since Mr. Nevin from the phone company had walked up to me twelve hours, or a hundred and fifty thousand years, ago.

* * *

Ferguson and Don both took the day off work and, with Rootbeer's help, we completely emptied the deli. The sooner we got the work done, the less chance there was of word getting back to Plotnick that he'd had a disaster. There had been nothing in the papers, and the police were hoping to keep it that way. The whole business didn't reflect very well on them.

The insurance adjustor arrived, and was so happy not to have to deal with Plotnick that we settled on the spot. As part of the big cover-up, the Police Department was paying in full, so all we had to do was clean, fix, and replace, and have the bills sent to the insurance company.

"It's a pleasure working with you guys!" exclaimed the adjustor in a surprised, pleased tone. "Mr. Plotnick is lucky to have you to look after his interests."

"Now, we don't want him informed about this," said Ferguson. "His health is very delicate."

"Hey," said the man, "no crying, no screaming, no begging, no groveling — I'll do anything you say."

"Okay," said the Peach as the adjustor drove off. "I guess now we go buy Plotnick his stuff back."

"Not exactly," I said. I can't describe the expression I was pretty sure I was wearing. Suffice it to say I was very, very excited about the rest of the summer.

"What do you mean, not exactly?" asked Don suspiciously. "Get that look off your face, Jason. You're making me nervous."

My leer must have deepened, because now they were both scared.

"Remember," warned Ferguson, "this is Plotnick's money. If you do something screwy with it, he'll track you to the end of the universe with bloodhounds!"

I laughed. "Trust me."

From *The Toronto Star*, Thursday, August 16, 1990:

GRAND OPENING TOMORROW
CHOCOLATE MEMORIES
1 Pitt Street at Bathurst
The Dessert that made the Olympiad Delicatessen
Famous is BACK!
Experience the Elusive Taste from your Past
in our authentic European Cafe
Best Deli Sandwiches in Town
Espresso, Cappuccino, Cafe au Lait
OPEN 4 P.M. TO 1 A.M.

I bombed out in plastics, I was useless at finding a job. All I had was my A in home ec, and now I was going to take my one talent and run with it.

The deli was dotted with tiny tables with checkered cloths, and seated well over a hundred now that all the booths were gone. So were the salamis and all of the old decorations, especially the hubcap playpen and Plotnick's monthly extermination certificate. Everything was painted white, and from the ceiling hung dozens of lush green plants. On the walls were framed posters of any European city whose consulate was giving them out for free.

The menu, written in fluorescent chalk on a large black slate over the counter, was much more limited than the Olympiad's had been. The Chocolate Memory had turned into about forty desserts, depending on what combination of ice cream, biscuit, fruit, and topping was used. For instance, with vanilla ice cream and cherries, it was Chocolate Memory Jubilee; with chocolate ice cream and crushed chocolate cookies and fudge sauce, it was Chocolate Memory Mississippi Mud Pie. And so on, right up to Chocolate Memory Rootbeer Racinette, which had everything, and would rival the Moontrix Mountain, the drink that had brought Jessica into all our lives.

We also served a few store-bought pastries and muffins, on the off-chance that someone didn't like Chocolate Memory. For dinner, we had deli sandwiches, period. It was the only thing Plotnick had really done well. And as a tribute to our injured landlord, I raised the prices of everything. Naturally people would expect to pay more in such a snazzy dessert spot. Your basic Chocolate Memory started at $3.50; the Rootbeer Racinette version was over seven bucks.

The former deli lay in readiness for tomorrow night's big opening, but there were still a few finishing touches to be put on the bathroom of apartment 2C. So I left Rootbeer in charge, and went to visit Plotnick at the hospital. My motive was not exactly social and compassionate. I wanted to make sure that our landlord's daily paper didn't include the ad for the opening of Chocolate Memories. All summer I'd never seen Plotnick so much as glancing at a newspaper, but I couldn't be too careful. Now, with nothing to do all day, he might have taken an interest in current events.

The nurse hadn't brought in his *Toronto Star* yet, so it was just sitting outside the door. I slipped out the Entertainment section and tossed it down the laundry chute. Then I put on my most cheerful face, and brought him the rest of his paper.

He took one look at me and screamed, "What are you doing here, Mr. Cardone? Who's minding the restaurant?"

"I closed up for an hour so I could come and visit you."

"Fine! You visited me! Go back! There could be a thousand-dollar catering job banging on my door right now!"

"Don't worry," I assured him. "I told Rootbeer to keep an eye on the place."

I didn't know the word "Oi" could have eighteen syllables.

"I brought you your paper," I said, placing it on the table beside him.

He glanced at it. "It's short one section. Those crooks."

I stared at him. "You read it?"

"Of course not!" he snapped. "I should waste my time reading a newspaper put out by crooks? Get out of here, Mr. Cardone! My business is going down the drain!"

I headed for the door, then paused. "Have any of the other tenants been in to visit you?"

Plotnick looked haughty. "My relationship with them is strictly business."

Translation: He was rotten to them, so they hated him just like we did. Good. That meant there was no danger of any of our neighbors telling Plotnick what was going on at 1 Pitt Street.

Opening night. I shouldn't have been nervous. My Chocolate Memory fans showed up in force, and only the Ugly Man missed the old menu. I guess it's hard to be nostalgic about all that grease. The place was never actually jam-packed, but it was probably the same number of people that had made the deli look like a sardine can last week. And I'm pretty sure I made more money than Plotnick had ever seen in an evening at the Olympiad. The customers seemed happy, which was the whole point.

Since it didn't count as a repair, I had taken out the newspaper ad with my own cash, and one night's tips had almost made up for it. I was still in the hole for my outfit — black pants, white shirt, black bow tie — but with luck, tomorrow would more than pay that off. I think I looked pretty sharp, and God's Grandmother said I was "all the crack," whatever that meant. Of course, none of my customers could know that I was much more than a mere waiter — that I was the mastermind behind Chocolate Memories. With a little bit of help from the D-Lishus Corporation.

The one thing I had looked forward to with dread was that first phone call from Plotnick on opening night. I'd already fielded one call from him in the morning, and had acted like it was business as usual at the Olympiad. I'd even pretended to be ringing up a check, because I knew the sound of the cash register was soothing to him. But now, would he be able to tell, with all his finely honed senses, that his restaurant was gone, and mine had risen from its ashes?

"I hear music, Mr. Cardone."

"The radio," I said. "Do you also hear a lot of people chewing?"

"It's that miserable rock and roll. It makes me crazy."

"Does it make you crazy that we're still crowded at nine o'clock?"

"I keep an open mind. Your houseguests, Mr. Peach and Mr. Champion, came to see me tonight. I'd forgotten how annoying they are. Funny how an old man doesn't remember."

I glanced at the blender through the kitchen door. A fresh batch of cake mix was ready. "I've got to go, Mr. Plotnick. It's very busy here."

"Go. Go in good health. Make money. You're a good boy."

That's twice I was a good boy. I said a prayer for the success of Chocolate Memories.

Business continued to be steady, and by early next week I was totally exhausted. There was no way I could continue to be cook, dessert chef, waiter, cashier, and maintenance man for a going concern like Chocolate Memories. Plotnick was making more than enough money to spring for another staff member, especially since I was working for nothing more than tips and glory.

The *Help Wanted* sign spent about forty-five minutes in our window before I had to interview my first applicant. Guess who?

"I *love* what you've done with the place," Jessica raved. "Do you know that whole neighborhoods have been known to turn on one or two little renovations like this?"

200

"Do you have any restaurant experience?" I asked, figuring I'd go through the motions before telling her to take a hike.

"Not really. But I learn fast, and I really need this job. To be honest with you, I'm bored now that Ferguson and Don won't go out with me anymore."

I stared. "They dumped you?" How could I have missed this development? Although, come to think of it, I hadn't heard them fighting lately.

"No, but they insist I have to choose between them, and I don't like to be ordered around."

Well, what do you know? While I'd been busy hawking cake mix, Ferguson and Don had developed pride. Now Her Royal Majesty, Jessica Lincoln, would have to have her boyfriends one at a time for a while, until she could find another pair of patsies.

"I don't think you'd like it here," I said hopefully. "You see, there's *work* — "

She hung her head. "I know. You kind of did my home ec for me. And you were fabulous, Jason."

"The pay's pretty lousy," I persisted, "but the tips are okay. The hours are hard, and there are no breaks . . ." And we flog you every night, and if you drop a glass, we feed you to the alligators in the basement. Please go away.

"I think I'd be a really good waitress," she went on, "because I work so well with people. Come on, Jason — *please!*" She gave me a lethal dose of lost puppy eyes.

So I took her out and got her a uniform just like mine, only with a skirt instead of pants, and so

201

ended my stint as the best-looking waiter at Chocolate Memories.

"Traitor!" was Don's opinion. Even the Peach looked a little disapproving. "She's supposed to be sitting at home, agonizing over her decision. Now you've got her slinging cake mix, having a great time, and she'll never get around to us."

"The summer's almost over, you know," Ferguson added resentfully.

But — surprise, surprise — she was a pretty good waitress, efficient, friendly, and hardworking. Between us we ran the place like clockwork. There was that one anxious moment when I came out of the kitchen to find Jessica picking up the phone, but I managed to grab it from her just in time. Plotnick should never hear a female voice answering his telephone: "Chocolate Memories."

"I get it," she smiled knowingly. "You want it to be a big surprise."

"Something like that," I replied. It was very important that, when Plotnick found out what I had done, he should be face to face with the happy reality of a successful restaurant and a full cash register. We were already responsible for his back injury; I didn't want anything to do with his cardiac arrest.

Business was good, but I knew it would take a special break to bump it up to the next level. Things were going as well as they could with word of mouth, my main form of advertising. Suddenly I found myself kind of disappointed by our current status. I spent my time at the blender contemplating Chocolate Memories' next quantum leap. Naturally the best thing would be a media blitz, but we couldn't afford that. Actually we could, but if Plotnick ever found out, I'd be mulched.

Jessica didn't understand my blue mood. "How much better could it be, Jason? Do you know how many places open up and never get near this successful?"

"I want people lined up down the block. I want it to be like Gourmet Week. What's so great about that guy Hamish?" Oh, no! Before, I was starting to think like my mother, and that was bad enough. Now I was thinking like — Plotnick!

Then, out of nowhere, came our big chance. *The Toronto Star* called and told us that, on Friday, they'd be sending a restaurant critic to review Chocolate Memories. We wouldn't know who or when, just that he'd be coming on Friday.

I freaked. Jessica and I washed every square inch of the restaurant. I had our shirts bleached and starched. I even replaced the plants that weren't doing well.

She was confident. "Relax, Jason. The place is great. We'll do fine."

"I don't know," I muttered. "It's okay, but there's got to be that one little something extra we can add that'll take us from a good place to a *great* place."

But what? Friday morning and afternoon I wracked my brain. Entertainment? No money, and no room. Food? I was lucky with the D-Lishus cake mix but, let's face it, I was no great chef. Decoration? I was no designer, either. A gimmick, a gimmick. Something different. And cheap.

It came to me five minutes before opening. Rootbeer's latest hobby was charcoal sketching, and he was pretty good at it, especially the portraits. He'd done one of Jessica that came out so realistic that Don and the Peach had fought over it, tearing it to shreds in the process. Wouldn't it add a sort of classy and artistic air to have a portrait artist working right in the restaurant? Nothing fancy, just Rootbeer in a quiet corner, sketching the customers. They could pay attention if they were interested; if not, it wouldn't bother them at all.

I phoned upstairs to Rootbeer and offered him a job drawing my patrons.

He was instantly wary. "You mean you want me to *work*?" You could just hear the burnout coming on.

I back-pedaled. "Of course not! Work? Ha-ha. Never. It's your hobby, which is the opposite of work."

He was still suspicious. "Are you sure?"

"Absolutely," I said, only vaguely aware that I might be risking Bad Luck if he saw through me. The restaurant was all that mattered. "You just do your hobby, like you normally would, only instead of doing it up there, you're doing it down here. Try it for one night."

"Well," he said, "okay."

Two minutes to four. There were already a few early birds waiting outside the door.

"Clear a spot in the corner," I called to Jessica, darting downstairs and coming back with one of Plotnick's old counter stools. "We've got a portrait artist. Guess who? Rootbeer!"

She was thrilled. "What a great idea!"

Only Rootbeer didn't show up. I called the apartment every ten minutes from four-thirty on, and there was nobody home. (Don was working the late shift at the theater, and Ferguson was in Chicago for Plastics Unlimited.) Then we got busy, and all I could do was berate myself as I waited on my customers. Why hadn't I been more specific? "Try it for one night," had been my exact words. But I'd forgotten to mention that the "one night" had to be *tonight*. What if the night he picked was in November, 1997? Rootbeer was like that. Here was such a great idea, and it was going to slip through my fingers because of a technicality! The guy from *The Star* would come and go, we'd get a mediocre review, and that would be it.

As the evening wore on, my black despair became just a dull ache. I stared long and hard into the face of every customer, trying to smoke out the reviewer so I could explain that our resident portrait artist was sick tonight. And couldn't he come back sometime to see how great it was? Like, maybe, November, 1997? Then I gave up on that, too. I didn't actually expect the guy to be wearing a flag that said "Restaurant Critic."

But then, at eleven o'clock, who showed up but Rootbeer Racinette. My hopes rekindled. Maybe the reviewer was still here! Chocolate Memories was full. I grabbed Rootbeer by the arm and began dragging him to his corner.

"Oh, Rootbeer, thank God!" Suddenly I noticed that he was carrying an enormous portable stereo cassette player. "What's that? Where's your easel?"

"You told me to do my hobby."

"Yeah, but your hobby is sketching, remember?"

"Not anymore," said Rootbeer.

And before I could stop him — not that I could anyway — he popped a tape in the deck and hit Play. Slow blues guitar came out of the speakers. There was a murmur from the crowd as all attention shifted to Rootbeer, who was swaying side to side to the music. Then he reached under his poncho, pulled out a shiny new harmonica, and began playing along with the tape — *with his nose*!

I *prayed* that the critic had already gone home to write a nice quiet review of a nice quiet place where nobody played the nasal harmonica. I stood rooted with horror to the spot until I heard Jessica whisper in my ear,

"Psst. I thought he was going to draw pictures."

I was bitter. "We talked about it," I whispered back, "and we decided *this* would be more appropriate!"

I couldn't take my eyes off him. It was disgusting, unsanitary, and gross! I mean, people were supposed to *eat* here! If this made the paper, I would have to do the honorable thing and fall on my meat fork.

But then the song ended, and Rootbeer got a standing ovation. Seriously. My first thought was *People are sick*. My second was *Gee, I hope the restaurant critic stayed around for this great show*.

The review was a rave. I have it framed on my wall, and I want to be buried with it. The desserts were "delicious," the decor "charmingly understated," the service "good," and the entertainment "unparalleled in its energy, inventiveness, and pure comic appeal. Anybody who doesn't go to catch the sweets and the show is crazy." I'll buy that.

Don and Ferguson went to the hospital to steal Plotnick's Entertainment section while I prepared for our biggest night ever.

I knew we were going to get a crowd, but nothing could have prepared me for what showed up on Saturday. Gourmet Week was an off-night by comparison. I pressed Ferguson and Don into service, and they were glad to be part of the excitement.

From about five o'clock on, the line stretched from the doorway to Bathurst Street and around the corner. We served cake mix until we were dropping, and Don and the Peach made no attempt to hide their openmouthed astonishment at this, the fruit of my chronic unemployment. The cash register rang like church bells.

To the delight of the crowd, Rootbeer came early. "Rootbeer," I said in concern, "where's the tape deck?" I didn't even need an answer. I knew exactly where it was — in the corner of our living room with the telescope, rocks, stamp collection, *et al.* A new hobby was about to be premiered.

Taking his place on the stool, he reached under the poncho and produced a ream of bond paper. The crowd waited expectantly. This was the hilarious entertainment they had heard so much about. He removed the top sheet, folded it painstakingly into an airplane, and sent it sailing over the tables.

That's it? Paper airplanes? I gasped. Was my glorious success at an end *so soon*?

With the undivided attention of every patron in

the place, Rootbeer made about fifteen of these airplanes and test-flew them. The people outside in line had their noses pressed up against the glass, watching in fascination.

The fifteenth plane landed nose first in Juliet's Chocolate Memory Banana Split. Painfully I signaled Jessica to make her a fresh one.

Finally one of the customers piped up, "Aren't you going to play the harmonica?"

"No," said Rootbeer honestly.

"Why not?" called someone else.

"I don't do that anymore." Then he went into his long speech about executive burnout. The audience stared at this woolly mammoth in a poncho lecturing them about stress, and decided that it must be a comedy routine. So they laughed. And once they got started, they were rolling in the aisles.

I was terrified Rootbeer would be insulted and start passing out Bad Luck. But he just returned to paper airplanes until another voice called, "Hey, there's a better way to make those."

So Rootbeer handed out paper, and everybody had a go at it. In no time at all, Chocolate Memories looked like the sky over O'Hare International Airport. It wasn't entertainment, exactly, but everyone seemed to be having a good time, and you can't argue with that. And the fun and games didn't cut into our take, either. People were ordering sandwiches, coffee, and desserts faster than ever.

Then the Peach made a paper airplane. It should be in orbit about now.

Thirteen

Plotnick's doctor said he could go home on Saturday, September 1st, to bid us an emotional farewell. I knew what the old stinker was really concerned about was getting his hands on the September rent, which we had to pay, according to my arrangement with Joe. My brother had already paid for our two weeks in June, and would refund the other half month when he got home.

Since the Olympiad Delicatessen, now a distant memory, didn't open till noon on Sundays, I was able to visit our landlord without him having a fit over why I wasn't in the deli.

The old man was in his usual rage. "They have two nurses here — the ugly one, and the uglier

209

one. It puts me off my food, which is okay, because it's poison."

I smiled. "So you're doing just fine."

He glared at me. "You're maybe deaf, Mr. Cardone? This so-called doctor — a more annoying person doesn't live. What would make me well is to work in the restaurant, where my whole life is."

My heart lurched. "Well, I guess I've got to go back and — uh — open — "

"Hurry up," ordered Plotnick. "My customers like their coffee on time."

But Plotnick probably wouldn't have recognized his customers anymore. They were young, trendy, and hip. We catered to silk suits, leather and chains, and neon minis. Long hair, short hair, facial hair, pink hair, blue hair, and no hair were all welcome. From the stock exchange to the loading docks came Chocolate Memories' clientele, bringing power ties and dog collars, and all shades of gray in between. None could seem to place the elusive flavor of our feature dessert, and all were united in a fever of admiration for the talents of Rootbeer Racinette.

That week, Rootbeer took up whittling, ant farming, calisthenics, shoe repair, and yodeling. This last was on Thursday, and it brought the house down. By this time, Don had quit his job at the theater, and was working for me again, which was okay, as long as he kept his flirting to a minimum. And even Ferguson came straight from the office to the restaurant every day. The Peach was the big genius, but we were out-earning him from our tips alone. We were getting customers from as far away as Montreal, Buffalo, and Detroit. Chocolate Memories was the hottest place in town.

There were tears in my eyes as we opened the doors at four o'clock on Friday, August 31st, and ushered in the first flood of customers, mostly business people who had left work early in order to get a seat. It was an emotional moment. Chocolate Memories would probably be around for a long time, but after tonight its mastermind had to go home and enroll in the twelfth grade. This was my last opening.

Who knew what direction Plotnick would try to take with his new restaurant? Jessica had lined up a couple of waiters to start tomorrow, and Rootbeer had vowed to continue the fight against executive burnout in public, so we weren't leaving Plotnick in the lurch. But if our landlord thought he could run this place by the meat fork, like he had the Olympiad, he was in for a shock.

The weekend crowds were always larger, and the line formed almost immediately. Ferguson was going to be late, as Plastics Unlimited was throwing him a giant farewell bash for his last day at work. So Jessica, Don, and I were running around like chickens with our heads cut off. Rootbeer showed up around five-thirty. His new hobby? Bubble blowing. The giant assumed his stool with an entire carton of chewing gum under his arm.

It was his most amazing performance to date. First he popped about ten pieces into his mouth and chewed for a few minutes. Then he jammed this wad behind his ear and started on another ten. As he chewed, cheeks moving like two dogs fighting under a blanket, he seriously informed the crowd that he wasn't going for the world record. That would be stressful, he said, and bubble blowing was a very relaxing hobby.

"But just in case I get it anyway, somebody better have a tape measure to witness it for the Guiness Book."

In the roar of appreciation that followed, I knew that if I slapped on a $100 surcharge per table, not one single person would leave. This was an event.

By the time Ferguson arrived around eight-thirty, Rootbeer had worked up his first really good bubble. It extended from his mouth like a second head, only bigger, bobbing slightly, thinning as it grew. Finally, his face an unhealthy shade of purple, he nodded at Jessica.

"Forty-eight and a half!" she called out, measuring the circumference at its widest point.

The audience howled its approval. It was well short of the record, which was seventy-three inches, but no one seemed to mind. Then the bubble burst, and there was Rootbeer, his entire head encased in a thin layer of pink gum. He got a standing ovation. Rootbeer didn't seem to mind the gunk matting his hair and beard. Instead, he looked with great annoyance at a tiny speck of gum stuck to the front of his poncho.

"I hate when stuff gets on my stuff!" Irritably he ripped off the poncho and threw it over the counter. It was just like washday. Debris rained all around him for thirty seconds. The crowd was in an advanced state of hysterics, but Rootbeer just popped more gum into his mouth and started on another wad.

It was non-average. The sight of Rootbeer bare-chested would have made a show in itself. Add layer upon layer of exploded bubbles from the top of his head to the buckle of his belt, and you had something these people were going to be telling their grandchildren. I was afraid that the combined weight of the standees outside in line, leaning four deep against the glass, would bust the show window. They came in in awe, they went out in awe, having eaten, laughed, and tipped lavishly. And as the bubbles gradually inched their way towards the record, I knew perfect contentment. It was a storybook ending to an amazing summer.

I was taking a breather, basking in this feeling, when I spotted Don backsliding on his promise. There he sat, at a corner table, in earnest conversation with a pretty redhead. The guy was a flirtaholic. Here, right at the moment of perfection, I was going to have to fire Mr. Wonderful *again* — and have him hate me all through the twelfth grade.

Squaring my shoulders, I began snaking my way through to Don, much to the annoyance of the customers who were concentrating on Rootbeer. I stopped short. That wasn't just *any* girl Don was nuzzling up to. It was Kiki. *The* Kiki.

How would Don react? My mind raced back to the hundreds of phone calls at all hours of the day and night; the endless fights with her "parents"; Mr. Nevins, and our panic the night of the shootout. Don was going to kill her! I strained to eavesdrop.

"You sent me on a wild goose chase!" Don was saying angrily. "You deliberately gave me a phony number, and I almost got busted!"

"I was going nuts!" she exclaimed, beaming up

at him. "The number isn't phony — it's right, but I'm not from Toronto — I'm just visiting! I forgot to give you the area code — 519!"

Don goggled, and so did I. "519? But that's — that's — "

"Have you ever been to Owen Sound?" she inquired innocently.

As it turned out, not only did Kiki live in the same town; she also lived ten minutes from Don's house. And when she found out he was Mr. Wonderful, the local hockey legend, I figured nothing could stop them.

Wrong again. There in the show window stood Kiki's father, face stony as ever, beckoning to his daughter.

"I have to go." Painfully she shook Don's hand, and made her way to the door, gazing back at Mr. Wonderful with every other step. She said, "Call me," and was gone.

I put my arm around Don's shoulders. "Well, what do you have to say to that?"

"The nerve of that girl!" he raged.

"What?"

"Where did she get off acting like Miss Big City Cool when she's really a small town hick?"

"You only talked to her for thirty seconds two months ago," I pointed out. "And besides, you do the same thing."

Mr. Wonderful folded his arms in front of him. "Just because it's the same doesn't mean it isn't different," he said smugly.

I groaned. "Fine. But hang onto her number. For my sake, okay? I have a feeling you're going to need it when this wears off."

Suddenly Don slapped his forehead. "Oh, no! I think I flushed it!" And with that, he shot out the front door and up to apartment 2C, in search of his napkin and his destiny. He returned, empty-handed and irritable, planning to knock on every door in his neighborhood until he found Kiki, starting September 2nd.

The ultimate bubble began at about ten o'clock. It was obvious from the start that this was the one that would catapult Rootbeer into history. He started it slowly, applying air steadily — not too quickly — and even in the early stages you could tell that the pink walls were thick and strong. The crowd fell into a hushed expectant silence as Rootbeer nurtured his masterpiece.

Jessica was terrified as she painstakingly held the tape measure around the humongous beach-ball-and-a-half that hung in front of Rootbeer. She knew that if she slipped, and burst what was very possibly the largest bubble in the history of man's life on Earth, she would be lynched by our patrons.

It took more than one tape measure length. Carefully she remembered her place, and started again from one. The result came quickly.

"Seventy-four and three-quarters!" Jessica shrieked.

Pandemonium broke loose. Our hundred-plus customers stood up on their chairs and screamed. For a moment I thought the ceiling would come down. I looked outside. There was dancing in the street. Rootbeer and his bubble rose carefully to acknowledge this ovation.

It was like New Year's Eve. People were slapping each other on the back, and kissing. Jessica was dancing on the counter, and I was locked in an ecstatic embrace with Don and the Peach. It was the first time all summer that we truly felt what this excursion was supposed to be all about — three friends taking on the world, and winning!

I didn't think anything could overpower the roar of the crowd, but something did. It was a half-demented voice, and it bellowed:

"WHERE'S MY RESTAURANT?"

I wheeled to face Plotnick, who stood in the middle of the room, quivering with rage.

Kapow! The record-breaking bubble could hang on no longer. It exploded all over Rootbeer. It was actually silent, but I heard the *kapow* in my mind.

Plotnick took in the scene. There stood Rootbeer, half naked, a woolly mountain of bubble gum. The hair on his head, face, chest, and arms was a mass of sticky pink. Then there was the crowd, which was out of control.

I ran over to Plotnick to comfort him in this moment of shock. He glared at me with malice.

"Mr. Cardone, I didn't recognize you! *Now* I recognize you! *You're the devil!* There are no words for such a terrible person what you are! You — you — you should grow like an onion with your head in the ground!"

There was no explaining — not in this chaos. So I figured I'd do it by show-and-tell. I dragged him over to the cash register and dramatically pressed the No Sale. The drawer popped open, an eruption of money. You know how, in Saturday morning cartoons, the characters' eyes bulge three feet out of their heads? That's what happened to Plotnick.

He stared at stray tens and twenties that fell like waste paper from the jammed trays. They came to rest on the metal strongbox that we kept under the counter. With a flourish, I opened it, too. Fort Knox.

In all the time I'd known him, I'd never seen Plotnick at a loss for words. He gawked for a while, his eyes caressing the treasure, and then looked up at me, the devil.

"Nobody can be all bad," he conceded.

And then he took over. I don't know where he found a greasy apron, because the laundry was freshly done, but he did. He hefted his meat fork, and smiled at me.

"You'll excuse me, Mr. Cardone. I have some freaks to straighten out." He walked right up to Rootbeer and *pushed him off the stool!* "Put your clothes on and get a job!" Then he turned his attention to my patrons.

"All right, you mutants!" he bawled, marching up and down like a fat drill sergeant. "This establishment is under new management! These are the rules! There will be no throwing up in this restaurant! You're going to see a lot of offensive degenerate things, and if it makes you crazy, you're out! Food goes from the plate to the mouth — nowhere else! And if you use filthy, disgusting, nasty language, I'm going to call your parole officers! Have a lovely evening."

I was in agony. After all my sweat making Chocolate Memories the best place in town, this ill-mannered old lout was going to insult the customers and ruin everything.

But then something weird happened. Instead of getting up and walking out, the crowd burst into laughter and applause.

"They think he's an act!" I blurted out.

"What else?" grinned the Peach. "Who'd believe there could be a guy like Plotnick?"

Since the customers stayed, we got back to work. Plotnick joined the waitering squad, serving coffee and dessert with all the grace and charm of a farmhand slopping the hogs.

"Okay, you Cossack, eat this if you can find your mouth!"

"He's so *cool*!" declared a skinhead, slipping Plotnick a big tip.

"You're a good boy, you know that?" beamed Plotnick. "Let me recommend a good vivisectionist for you."

The new proprietor was an instant hit. And since Rootbeer was in the kitchen trying to get the bubble gum out of his hair, Plotnick was called to the corner for an encore presentation of The Rules. He was glad to oblige, and went on for twenty minutes about such topics as how to use a knife and fork, what is a bathroom and why do I need one, and when and where not to commit violent crime.

The crowd was convulsed with hilarity when Plotnick interrupted his lecture and stood still as a statue, nose twitching. A hush fell, and outside, the squeal of tires could be heard. Plotnick raced into the kitchen, and there was the sound of wild scrambling, and things being tossed around.

"Mr. Cardone, where is it? *Where is it?*"

"In the corner with the broom!" I called back.

A second later, he burst out, carrying his trusty

butterfly net. Waving it at face level to clear a path for himself, he barreled out the door just as a sports car hit the pot hole on Bathurst Street. A month in traction had done nothing to dull his reflexes. The hurtling hubcap found the net like a homing pigeon.

Chocolate Memories went berserk.

Still on the sidewalk, slightly out of breath, Plotnick examined the hubcap with evident pleasure. Then he stood in the doorway and made his announcement.

"Okay, out!"

At first, no one took him seriously. But when he started prodding people with the butterfly net, they got the message. They still thought it was part of the show, so there was a lot of laughing and cheering as they filed out, pausing to congratulate Plotnick and pat him on the back.

"Go home!" he told them. "You're bringing down the property values!"

They remained a little longer on the sidewalk outside 1 Pitt Street, giving our landlord one last round of applause. Then they gradually dispersed.

He turned to us, the staff. "Go to bed. I'm having an ulcer."

"Oh, sure, Mr. Plotnick." I grinned. "You just want to be alone to dive into that cash box."

"I have to hide, Mr. Cardone. That fascist doctor could be coming after me any minute. I'm not supposed to be out till tomorrow." He checked the clock. "Ah! It *is* tomorrow. The first of the month. That'll be $685, please."

We stared at him. "Mr. Plotnick!" I cried. "Is that all you can think about after what you've seen here tonight? We've all worked like crazy to make this place a success for you!"

Plotnick shrugged. "I don't want no deadbeats in my building."

I was furious. "You'd better be nice to us! We're the only ones who know the secret recipe for the Chocolate Memory, which is the backbone of the whole menu!"

Plotnick reached over and dipped a pudgy finger into a half-finished dessert. He licked at it experimentally. "Big deal. Cake mix."

Where money is involved, Plotnick is always right. When Plotnick is wrong, see above. We wrote him a check. At least this time we could afford it.

Out on the sidewalk, Ferguson and Don confronted Jessica.

"All right," said Don, "you've dodged us for a whole summer, made us look like idiots, and almost turned two friends against each other." Ferguson nodded feelingly. "Now we've got something to say to you. We want you to know that we don't care who you would have picked. In fact, we couldn't care less. Right, Peachfuzz?"

"Right," the Peach confirmed. "It doesn't interest us in the slightest."

"But I've made my choice," she said.

They both leaned forward tensely.

"I pick — Jason."

She picked *Jason*? Since when was I one of the choices? This was the girl who went out of her way to date everybody I knew *except* me!

"Hah!" Don slammed his fist into his palm. "Jason's with us. He wouldn't stab his friends in the back. Would you, Jason?"

My eyes were glazing over. I started having lightning visions — Jessica at the supermarket; casserole day; the seven-day menu. Sure, she'd always run off at the end, but that was a mad dash for class. Come to think of it, for a girl with not one but two boyfriends, she'd hung around me a lot. And coming to work at Chocolate Memories — she hadn't needed a job before. She must have been trying to get close to me!

Don tapped me on the shoulder. "Would you, Jason?"

"Uh — uh — no," I said feebly.

She shrugged. "Oh, well. No hard feelings. It's been nice meeting you guys. Have a good trip home." Then she turned and headed for Bathurst Street.

She picked Jason! All this time she'd been trying to get through to me. But everything she'd said or done had just made me madder. I was so jealous and resentful at being third choice — worse! *no* choice! — that I'd missed what was right in front of my nose!

She picked Jason.

And tomorrow Jason was going back to Owen Sound, and she might as well have picked Plotnick. It was a masterstroke of stupidity best summed up in three words: I blew it.

Mr. Wonderful and the Peach were slapping each other on the back, talking about solidarity and how " . . . we showed her!" But I was rooted to the spot, watching Jessica disappear around the corner. I wanted to throw myself to the pavement, kicking and screaming.

Then they must have caught a glimpse of the look on my face, because suddenly, Don gave me a shove.

"What are you standing here for, you moron? If you run, you can still catch her."

Ferguson pushed, too. "Don't approach her from behind," he advised. "Go wide out and cut in front."

I ran like crazy.

It must have been four A.M., and it might have been a dream, but I don't think so. The quiet on Pitt Street was shattered by a half-demented voice in the street below.

"Yoo-hoo! Hamish! *Eat your heart out!*"

Fourteen

We said good-bye to all our neighbors, and even had a chat with the Phantom through his closed door. God's Grandmother made us a package of sandwiches to eat on the train.

At the bank, we cleaned out our joint account. With the success of Chocolate Memories, we were taking home over $700, plus the half-months' rent we'd be getting back from Joe. Not bad for three guys whose parents had been expecting them to come crawling home in bankruptcy on Day Two.

Don grabbed the bank draft out of my hands. "This goes towards getting us back to Toronto next summer."

I stared at him. "You mean you'd come back, after all we've been through?"

"Well, of course!" roared Mr. Wonderful. "Sure, we had a few problems, but we improvised, we side-stepped, we overcame. That's living!"

Ferguson nodded in agreement. "This was the only way to spend the summer. I was wrong, and you guys were right."

Don threw an arm around him. "Welcome to Planet Earth, Peachfuzz. It took a long time, but you finally realized there's more to life than Stonehenge. I never thought I'd say this, but I like you!"

"I *have* to come back next year," Ferguson added. "Plastics Unlimited is flying me down in their jet. If I work for them every summer, they're going to pay my way through Harvard and start me as a junior vice-president."

"Liking you is going to be harder than I thought," said Don through clenched teeth.

"I'll be down here before you guys," I said casually. "Visiting Joe and — you know — uh — " I reddened. " — Jessica."

They looked at me pityingly.

"Peachfuzz and I are willing to overlook your temporary insanity this time, Jason," said Don. "Just don't expect such special treatment ever again."

Rootbeer, his beard still patchy-pink, was loading our luggage into the Camaro so he could drive us to the train station. He slammed the trunk shut and squeezed into the driver's seat. "I hate following train schedules. It puts you under so much stress."

"We'll be okay," Ferguson assured him. "There's plenty of time."

Plotnick appeared at the door of Chocolate Memories to wish us *Bon voyage*. "Ah, good-bye, Mr. Cardone, Mr. Champion, Mr. Peach. It seems like only yesterday you first arrived. It won't be the same without you."

"Sure," I said sarcastically. "Now you'll have to pay real waiters."

The landlord was undaunted. "I feel like you're my own children. You're three beautiful boys for doing such wonderful things for an old man."

I sighed. "Good-bye, Mr. Plotnick. It's been real."

"One last thing," said Plotnick as we all climbed into the car. "If you should see your brother before I do, tell him he has till September 30th to move out."

"*What?* We paid the rent, remember?"

"Certainly. For September. Then, on October 1st, I'm going into partnership with my oldest and dearest friend, Hamish. We're going condominium."

My mouth dropped open. "Condominium?!"

"This is a very fashionable neighborhood, Mr. Cardone. Chocolate Memories is right here on Pitt Street. It's a disgrace for a broken-down old building like this to be so close to such a fancy night spot."

"But — we can't lose that apartment!"

"Don't worry, Mr. Cardone. Your brother will have first pick of the new condominiums. Prices start at $150,000. Tell your brother to see Hamish. He'll like him. A prince of a fellow."

I was really steaming. This was the last straw. We'd been polite and respectful to that grease-spattered, potbellied, meat-fork-toting crook for the last time! *"Mr. Plotnick, you're a — "*

Rootbeer stepped on the gas, and the Camaro roared away, leaving my last sentence unfinished. It's a good thing, too. It never would have gotten by the censors.

SEPTEMBER

Fifteen

"That's the most ridiculous story I've ever heard in my life!" snarled Joe, marching up and down our living room in Owen Sound, practice-swinging an aluminum baseball bat. The image was clear. In the path of that bat could be one, two, or all three of our heads if Joe got any madder.

Ferguson, Don, and I were flaked out on the floor, frantically scouring all three Toronto newspapers for a new apartment for my brother.

"But it's all true, Joe! Every last word! You talked to Plotnick! We didn't get you evicted! He's going condo!"

"And whose fault is that?" roared Joe. "You couldn't be satisfied with living in the city! You had to fool around with cake mix, and show my rotten landlord how much money he could make with that dump!''

''But I explained that.''

''You lost the apartment! There's no explanation! Keep looking! You find me a place, or else!''

I turned back to the paper, and Joe continued his swinging, the bat whirring menacingly through the air. I wondered why I was so afraid of him. After the things I'd seen and done this summer, Godzilla shouldn't have scared me, let alone one puny bodybuilder. The guy who'd slept on our floor for two months was twice as big and twenty times as strong. Joe Cardone was a relatively minor hazard, like being afraid of broken pavement because you might turn your ankle.

''Here's a pretty good deal in the suburbs,'' ventured Ferguson. ''One bedroom, air conditioning — ''

''Forget the suburbs!'' interrupted Joe. ''You lost downtown, you find downtown!''

''Downtown's pretty expensive,'' commented Don.

''Of course it's expensive! That's why I wanted to keep the place I already had! But no — I had to have a dessert chef for a brother, and *he* had to have two stupid friends!''

I suppose we could have defended ourselves a little better. For instance, we might have pointed out that Joe could have caught a later flight, and stayed to give us a thorough briefing instead of that stupid message. Also, he could have phoned us a couple of times from Europe to ask how things were going, and give us a number to reach him in case of emergency. All we got were pictures of him lugging girls around beaches. But you don't say things like that to Joe Cardone when he's armed with a bat, and you're armed with *The Toronto Star*.

It seemed so unfair, after all our scrambling and struggling and sweating to keep Plotnick happy and save that apartment, to be accused of losing it because we were stupid. In that one summer, we'd fought for that place more than Joe ever had the whole time he'd lived there. If we hadn't been on our toes, the apartment would have been lost ten times! We were heroes! It had taken a reconciliation between Plotnick and his worst enemy in the world to get that lease from our protective custody! We hadn't done *one thing wrong*!

I was about to voice these thoughts to Joe when there was a cry of shock from Don. "Hey, look!" He grabbed the page of ads from Ferguson's hands, and turned it around. There, under the headline *Off-beat Comic Behind Bars* was a picture of our Rootbeer, smiling serenely out the grill-covered window of a paddy wagon.

"It's Rootbeer!" I said lovingly, remembering a few tight spots where Rootbeer had been our hairy fairy godfather.

Don began to read:

" 'Rootbeer Racinette, the new-wave comedian who's been wowing audiences at Toronto's Chocolate Memories, was arrested by police yesterday for running an illegal gambling operation. The exact nature of the offense has not been released, but officers confiscated a two-by-four and an undisclosed amount of cash. Racinette, who holds the world record for the largest chewing-gum bubble, is expected to be released on his own recognizance later today.' "

Ferguson grabbed the paper from Don, and continued, " 'Chocolate Memories, the popular dessert spot that housed Racinette's meteoric rise to fame, has been shut down by court order, pending resolution of a $1.5 million lawsuit by the D-Lishus Corporation. D-Lishus claims that its popular chocolate cake mix was unlawfully pirated by the restaurant. Chocolate Memories declined comment, but an anonymous inside source was quoted as saying, "D-Lishus is a bunch of low-class bums for pestering an old man." ' "

We laughed, and even Joe thought it was a little bit funny.

I ripped the paper away from the Peach, and finished the article.

" 'Racinette, twenty-three, should have no shortage of opportunities for his unique talents now that Chocolate Memories is in suspended animation. Offers for North American tours have been flooding in, although the six-foot-ten comedian denies that he has considered any of them. "I'm under too much stress to think about that kind of stuff. Maybe Joe Cardone will come back from Europe and be my manager." ' "

Joe let out a holler that was pure joy. The murderous look on his face was replaced by a goofy grin. "He wants *me* to be his manager!" he chuckled. "That's fantastic!"

"It couldn't have happened without Chocolate Memories," I was quick to point out. "I think you have something to say to your dessert chef brother and his two stupid friends."

"All right, sorry I blew my stack," he mumbled. "Hey, I don't even need an apartment. I'm going on tour! Good old Rootbeer."

My brother was in ecstasy. He threw down the bat and began to pace around the house. "Think of it — New York, L.A., San Francisco . . ."

As Joe continued to list all the great cities they'd tour, my eyes met Ferguson's and Don's. It was like Joe was the little kid, and we were the older brothers now. Success wasn't measured in particulars. It was the big picture that counted. You go to Toronto for the summer, and you make it through alive. All the rest is just details.

It was about a week later. When I came home from school, my mother was baking a cake.

"Want to lick the spoon?" she offered.

"Get real, Mom," I replied. "I'm past all that now."